SHADOW OF THE HEART

Shadow SEALs

SHARON HAMILTON

SHARON HAMILTON'S BOOK LIST

SEAL BROTHERHOOD BOOKS

SEAL BROTHERHOOD SERIES
Accidental SEAL Book 1

Fallen SEAL Legacy Book 2

SEAL Under Covers Book 3

SEAL The Deal Book 4

Cruisin' For A SEAL Book 5

SEAL My Destiny Book 6

SEAL of My Heart Book 7

Fredo's Dream Book 8

SEAL My Love Book 9

SEAL Encounter Prequel to Book 1

SEAL Endeavor Prequel to Book 2

Ultimate SEAL Collection Vol. 1 Books 1-4 /2 Prequels

Ultimate SEAL Collection Vol. 2 Books 5-7

SEAL BROTHERHOOD LEGACY SERIES
Watery Grave Book 1

Honor The Fallen Book 2

BAD BOYS OF SEAL TEAM 3 SERIES
SEAL's Promise Book 1

SEAL My Home Book 2

SEAL's Code Book 3

Big Bad Boys Bundle Books 1-3

BAND OF BACHELORS SERIES

Lucas Book 1

Alex Book 2

Jake Book 3

Jake 2 Book 4

Big Band of Bachelors Bundle

BONE FROG BROTHERHOOD SERIES

New Year's SEAL Dream Book 1

SEALed At The Altar Book 2

SEALed Forever Book 3

SEAL's Rescue Book 4

SEALed Protection Book 5

Bone Frog Brotherhood Superbundle

BONE FROG BACHELOR SERIES

Bone Frog Bachelor Book 0.5

Unleashed Book 1

Restored Book 2

SUNSET SEALS SERIES

SEALed at Sunset Book 1

Second Chance SEAL Book 2

Treasure Island SEAL Book 3

Escape to Sunset Book 4

The House at Sunset Beach Book 5

Second Chance Reunion Book 6

Sunset SEALs Duet #1

Sunset SEALs Duet #2

THE GUARDIANS

Heavenly Lover Book 1

Underworld Lover Book 2

Underworld Queen Book 3

Redemption Book 4

FALL FROM GRACE SERIES

Gideon: Heavenly Fall

NOVELLAS

SEAL Of Time Trident Legacy

All of Sharon's books are available on Audible, narrated by the talented J.D. Hart.

ABOUT THE BOOK

A man broken by service to his country…
Betrayed by the system who trained him…
A chance at a HEA gone forever, her life slipping through his fingers…

She was going to be Brady Rogers' forever woman, but she was lost to him thanks to sex traffickers who kidnapped her mission group in Mexico five years ago. After six months pouring over intel, he'd found her but was prohibited from engaging with the enemy by a fresh OIC, Lt. Rolland Stanley, straight out of the Academy via the Hamptons.

Ordered to stand down, he'd taken a round to the hip by sniper fire. Plagued by painful night sweats and seething with thoughts of revenge, he later discovers she'd been murdered in a bloody cartel turf war the next year.

Brady just barely completes his twenty and retires to the green triangle of Northern California to raise his CBDs off the grid, hoping to heal his physical as well as mental pain, but prepared to die in a shootout with the local authorities if it came to that.

He'd done his duty and felt his life was basically over.

Being antisocial wasn't a problem. He knew he was a danger to everyone, and he could just cruise through life in a hazy fog until that day…

But imagine his surprise when a strange woman calls and tells him Esquivel Rojas, the cretin who took Maggie's life, was also now living in California. Would he like the opportunity to cap that story? Hell, he didn't need the ginormous amount of money they were offering him for the live capture.

His biggest problem was going to be bringing in his prey *alive*!

Find out all the clues that lead to this warrior's satisfying ending in this action-packed thriller, full of cartels, comrades, and traitors. If you dare!

AUTHOR'S NOTE

This is dedicated to all those who have loved once, twice, perhaps three times or more, and thought they should give up. I believe in Happily Ever Afters. I believe in long slow kisses and moonlit strolls on the beach. I believe in walks in the woods on sunny days. I believe in forgiveness and the healing power of true love.

Love hurts and makes us strong at the same time. I believe it brings us to the truest expression of ourselves, and when we strive for true love, we are striving for the very best within our souls.

Yes, even for Navy SEALs, *True Love Heals in the Gardens of the Heart.*

No, not everyone gets an HEA. No, not every relationship can be saved, just as not every life can be spared when found in harm's way. But in my books, I try to show what could happen. And yes, I know the difference between reality and fiction, but I also know where I like to live.

Live well and love often. And let's explore the depths our hearts can take us, even in this very short ride of life.

—Sharon Hamilton

CHAPTER 1

MAGGIE'S RED HAIR draped defiantly off the side of the bed as her deep rose lips inhaled the lifegiving oxygen of her fiercely feminine side, her chest rising and falling to the command of her breath. She was a woman of contrasts, her sweet sleep disguising the fiery soul filled with stubborn "No's." The first time she'd told him "No," he'd known he'd wait forever for her to change her mind.

Forever. It would only be a long time if he managed to stay alive, another thing he didn't expect.

Brady was her devoted servant—marked, scarred, and tatted to the extreme, like most the other brothers on his SEAL Team—but his heart was branded with the invisible M he carried deep inside. If they opened him up some day when his warrior days were over, they'd see her initial emblazoned on his still cold heart, a fire letter to be sure, complete with its own energy field unextinguished by death no matter how much they carved up his carcass. That M would remain, just as his love for this woman would never end.

A man of few words and little expectations, he never saw himself falling in love or imagined a life with a soft goddess at his side, someone to take his mind off the wars he'd fought and the battles he'd struggled and won, inside as well as outside his huge well-toned cyborg of a body. He was a man-killing, dangerous sort of beast who might eat a vanquished man's heart in a macabre victory celebration like his Viking ancestors if the Navy hadn't injected some human decency and mental body armor to quell his self-destructive side. Before Maggie, all he sought was a good death.

He wanted to ride her body again, the two of them streaking across a desert plain in perfect sync, her flawless peachy skin held like precious treasure in his gnarled and twisted fingers, that smooth flesh ripe and ready to be tasted, squeezed, and then smoothed over with his sandpaper palms. Every time they made love, he was her conquering hero, come to fully enjoy the fruits of their love, his reward for removing the battle armor and allowing just one person in the whole universe to enter and see the real man inside.

There would only be one Maggie, one woman. First, there was none. Then, in a miracle, there was one but only one.

She loved with stubborn determination to keep up

with him, to embrace the throne he'd created for her, his warrior princess to rule over all time, long after his ashes were thrown into the sea. She would rule over all the hearts of heaven after his death, and she would never cease to be. She would defy death itself.

With one large claw, he spread his fingers over her bulging right breast, then arched her back beneath her shoulder blades with his other hand, serving her up to his hungry mouth. He placed his belly against hers, as his lips and tongue violated her nipple, waking her to arousal, his warrior maiden, while he felt the rumble of her moan all the way down to his root.

She'd told him many times that just his gaze upon her created a clothing malfunction of epic proportions. Those quick and urgent dashes to any platform where he could ram himself inside her sweet channel and ride her hard until they both lay exhausted were the high-lights of his days and dreams.

She flirted around the edge of her orgasm as he coaxed her, whispered things to her he could feel back in the sudden rapid beat of her heart. When he whis-pered, "Dear sweet Beloved, I am yours," he meant it with every cell of his body. He wanted her to shelter and grow inside her tender belly his sons and beautiful daughters to share the seasons of life with, to send him to Valhalla a happy man. He fucked with the art of legacy, the possibility of miracles, and the future he never deserved.

Maggie's form turned. Her smile became seared in his memory, her eyes fixed on him then on the wall behind him as he moved his head to the side to indulge a tender kiss to her long, fragrant neck.

That's when it started to change. The little serpent of regret coiled in his belly in a flash before her image dissipated into a cloudy peach mirage, expanding until the form was lost. His rod throbbed from unfulfilled passion, and he groped the bed sheets. Sweat poured down the ridge in his back along his spinal column.

"No!" he screamed to her. Then he begged in his silent, lover's voice, "Don't go. Stay with me, Maggie. Just a little while longer. I can bring you back. Return to me, my beloved."

But it was no use. The bright morning had turned cold. The only heat remaining was in his groin, his forehead, and, yes, the M emblazoned on his heart. He could hear the hiss as the brand seared deeper into his chest cavity.

Exhausted, he fell onto his backside. Opening his eyes to the wooden ceiling of his hideaway in the foothills of Northern California, he knew he was even more dangerous than before.

Brady waited until his breathing became normal, refusing to do one of the mind control techniques the Navy doctors had taught him. He even rejected the poses and meditation his yoga master lovingly demonstrated. His thoughts were filled with torching his bed with a flamethrower and, in one sweeping stroke, eliminating the source of pain: the bed that no longer smelled of Maggie. It was the same mattress they'd worshiped each other's bodies on in San Diego for a whole glorious year, before the events that took her away from him forever.

Tate, former Master Chief Brady Roger's huge black Doberman, came to the bedroom, stopped at the doorway, and sat with a small howl like he'd located a cactus needle in his butt. The dog was his protector now, government issue, but the one thing he was given after his nearly dishonorable discharge that he held onto. If he was being honest, clung to.

"Fuck, Tate. I'm okay. Just another goddamned dream. And no, she's not coming back. But fuckit, I sure tried this time. I got real close."

Tate angled his head as if in full comprehension. That little nod of the head, the quiet way he respectfully approached his master, the concern only a canine could have for such a fucked-up human being was Brady's lifeline now.

That and the CBD he grew in his garden.

"Come here, boy," he commanded the dog, who dutifully jumped on the bed and took up the space beside him. His paws pushed on Brady's stomach and thigh, smarting a bit. He was sure it was Tate's way of showing that, contrary to what Brady thought, the old SEAL was the owner, but Tate was the owner's master.

He scratched around Tate's ears as the hundred-pound dog laid his snout on Brady's chest.

"Another day in paradise, right, Tate?" he said to the dog, who licked his hand when he briefly stopped the ear scratching. "You got any plans today, boy?"

The dog placed his snout back on Brady's chest.

"Me neither. Just another fuckin' day. Maybe we'll check our little grow down by the creek, see if we can shoot a trespasser, huh? You'd like that, wouldn't you?"

Brady laughed. He hadn't caught one yet. A trespasser, that is. He'd caught lots of unsuspecting deer and even a wild boar trying to rut his way through his grow and paying for it with his life. He was a tasty motherfucker, Brady ruminated. Tate enjoyed some ribs even though he wasn't supposed to have them, served raw for his own protection. He devoured the bones as fast as the mulberries he liked to eat off the old tree that had fallen over during one of the storms but refused to quit bearing fruit while lying on its side.

But the truth was, Brady was itching to kill someone. He was going to have to wait until he got the opportunity. After all, the man was still a Naval officer.

Brady lurched up out of bed, even scaring Tate, and headed for the shower to get rid of his giz-soaked shorts and sticky groin area. He was disgusted as he tugged at the wet cotton embellished with red, white, and blue stars—another habit he'd procured from the Navy that was hard to break.

Tate sat on the shorts without comment, watching Brady shower, waiting for his turn to have his needs met. Minutes later, he was rewarded with fresh bison and beef with some kibble and allowed outside to wander for a private spot to use as a privy. Brady took his coffee with him, sat on the back deck, and surveyed his little plot of serenity—if that was the right word for it. Because there was no real serenity present.

He hadn't stopped drinking, smoking shit, or going overboard on the CBD oil. All these things both blew up and helped his nightmares. His hands were steadier, and his shot was truer now. He was able to do math, calculate stress loads and angles in his bridge building endeavors, and create creek-side trails for his cultivation out of prying eyes, which was a complete lie now with the drones the sheriff and special agents used these days. But he fantasized he was still nearly off the grid, even in this age of facial recognition and God-knew-what chips they must have inserted into him during his active days. He wiped the worry out of his head with the pleasant thought they knew he'd enjoy taking target practice on anyone who came wanting to fuck with him no matter who they were or who sent them. There was only one person he'd ever allow to live who could cross his log-hewn bridge with the boobytraps laced all around. And she was dead.

The rest of the world could fuck off.

He heard buzzing nearby as he scanned for Tate's poop plot he'd want to clean up later in the day. He thought it was an overgrown mosquito at first because his cell phone never rang. Never gave him updates. He'd punched a guy's lights out one day in a bar when he explained he only kept it in case his dead fiancé called him from heaven, and the guy laughed at him.

Brady had stuck two hundred dollars into the guy's shirt pocket as the stranger splayed out on the barroom floor, unconscious.

"That's to take care of his teeth," he said as he pointed to the bloody puddle containing a couple of pieces of white ivory floating like sailboats on the San Diego Bay. He guessed later the bartender warned the poor victim not to seek further compensation because Brady would more than likely kill him next time and wouldn't care.

It buzzed again, and yes; it was a call. But it wasn't from Heaven. The woman's voice wasn't Maggie's.

"Chief Rogers?" she said, sounding too familiar for her own health.

"Don't fuck with me. The answer is no. I don't want it."

"Want what?" she asked.

"Whatever it is your peddling."

"Oh, you're going to want to hear what I have to say, Chief."

"Do I know you?"

"Hell no."

She swore like she wasn't used to doing it. Brady wasn't impressed. He hit the disconnect and tucked the phone back into his pocket.

But the phone rang again.

"I said no the first time. There isn't anything you can say that will make me—"

"We found Esquivel Rojas."

Brady thought he was hallucinating again. He wasn't having a good time this revolution, either.

"I'd like to see a picture of his body please, riddled with holes, perhaps an eye or two carved out of his skull. Miss, what's your name?"

"That's not important. What's important is that he's alive and living in California. Less than a day's drive from you."

"You don't know where I live."

"You have a black Doberman named Tate who—"

"Shut up and quick fucking with me."

"I'm giving you a second chance to complete a mission. Well, perhaps not the mission the Navy sent you on before, but the mission in your mind, Chief Rogers."

The way she called him Chief made his skin go prickly. It was like the skin of his old dead Navy SEAL body he had to wear as camouflage to defy detection.

"Go on," he said.

"Good. I'm glad I have your attention."

"Lady, don't assume anything about me or I might just find out the name of your dog and come kill him."

"Teddy."

"What?"

"My dog's name is Teddy. But I doubt you'll find me."

"Is that a challenge?"

"Only one you'd be stupid to follow, and, Chief, you're not a stupid man. In fact, you're a very smart man who was wronged. I'm about to make that right. And I'm about to pay you a bounty for delivery of this cretin to us for a—"

"Who's us?"

"Don't you want to know how much I'm offering?"

"Are you kidding? I'd do it for free. Bet you didn't think about that, did you? No, the important thing is who you represent. Are you government or private, and if you're private, are you part of a criminal organization or rival gang?"

"I'm the one who is offering you a million dollars for his return. And I can guarantee you'll never serve time for the 'crime,' if you want to call it that. Some don't feel kidnapping someone who has caused so much tragedy and pain to so many people a crime. I represent a group of individuals you will never meet, never know, but who will pay you to do it."

"Why me?"

"Because you have a good reason. He was the one responsible for Maggie's kidnapping and ultimate murder. You have passion for the job, on top of your skill level, your focus, your reputation, and your score to settle. I'm betting you like to settle scores cleanly. This is the way you can do that. We'll be allies for a short period of time, and then we'll never hear from each other again."

"I won't do it unless I know who the 'we' is."

"Then I'm sorry. But the job will be assigned to someone else." The silence felt like a movie theater in pitch black with no one else in the room. Just Brady.

The old Brady would have hung up. She probably knew that. Maybe she half expected it. She was smart enough not to make a sly comment about it.

"What's my guarantee I'm working for the good guys?"

"There is only my word. My bond. But you'll have the satisfaction of finding him and settling the score with your past."

"I don't care about myself."

"That's the lie you tell yourself, Chief Rogers. But there is one catch, if you accept the job."

"Here it comes."

"Yes. Here it comes. My only condition. You notice I said kidnap. He can be bloodied, beat up a little. He can't have missing arms, legs, eyes, or even ears. You can perhaps take a trophy tat or two, but that's all. He has to be delivered alive."

Brady wasn't sure that feat was even possible.

CHAPTER 2

B RADY HAD TWO days of waiting before the first $50,000 was deposited to his account. Normally, he would've chucked the idea after twenty-four hours, but a million dollars was a million dollars, and the man he was supposed to capture was probably the only man in the world Brady ever wanted to see again, dead or alive. And he preferred to see him dead.

But there it was. The $50,000 sat all fat, chubby, and round in his bank account. He could hardly believe the numbers sprawled on his computer screen. He had never had that much money at one time, even when he got his signing bonus the last time he reupped onto SEAL Team 5.

Just to be sure, Brady called the bank and asked how much cash was available. The nice young teller pertly answered him back that it all was available since it had been a direct transfer from another account at the same bank.

"You mean they bank at the same bank that I do, here, in Healdsburg?"

"No, Mr. Rogers, I didn't mean to imply that. They bank with Four Seasons, just like you do, but I'm afraid I'm not allowed to tell you where the account was opened. Most importantly, they have an account with us. Therefore, it was just an electronic transfer."

He was going to say something smart but decided against it, mumbling to himself. The teller asked him to repeat what he just unintelligibly spoke, and he hung up.

What was it about being alive currently in the history of the world, all this electronic shit, all this bank electronic crap, all this efficiency, anonymity, danger, and whatever all the rest of it was?

Did I just sign up for some horrible terrible mission—a mistake I'll regret for the rest of my life?

He hoped the answer to that was no, but after all, he was a Navy SEAL by profession, at least he used to be. After twenty years working hard on the Teams, retiring as a Master Chief, he'd seen pretty much everything there was to see, until now. The world was a strange place. Made stranger each day. This mission was going to be no exception.

So the money was real, even though the people he was working for were not. Was it really any different than working for the government? Maybe they were the government. Maybe they were the same goddamn bureaucrats and head slammers he used to do dangerous things for, except now they just didn't want to show their faces or let him know who they were. Now he was going to possibly risk his life for some entity he didn't know much about. But when it came right down to it, he didn't know much about his own government anyway. He had never had a problem before doing it. This was the same thing.

Or was it?

Since the money was real, it was time for him to get real too. There was no way in hell he'd be able to go after Esquivel, not with his cadre of bandidos around him. He didn't want to be gunned down in a firefight with the man, who would literally dance a jig on his grave. That wouldn't be a very smart way to operate. Besides the goal was to get his satisfaction and seek his revenge for the death of Maggie. The hardest part, of course, was going to be delivering him alive to whoever the hell this woman worked for.

So it was time to give his old buddy Riley, the best gadget guy he ever worked with on Team 5, a call.

Riley had given him his address, but now Brady wasn't sure he'd be able to find it. He scrolled through his phone, and sure enough, he did still have the guy's number. He prayed it was still the same.

"Bones!"

"That's right, it's me. I know. Don't tell me. I told you I'd never call you again. I meant it then, but I got something I'm working on now. And I need to talk to you in person."

"Well, today's not a good day, Brady. We got stuff going on here at the house."

A toddler screamed in the background. He wasn't very versed in such things. As a matter of fact, he made sure he stayed as far away from kids, women, and especially babies as possible. Dogs? Well, that was something else.

He knew he was going to have to go travel to wherever Riley was, and he hoped to God the man didn't have cats. Brady was allergic to them, and it wasn't very manly to be having an asthma attack when you're a big guy, a former team guy like Brady was.

"So where the hell are you living? And that rug rat in the background, is that yours?"

"Better be. I think so. You haven't met my better half."

"Nope. I never was that kind of guy, Riley. You know that. I don't send cards, and I don't call on birthdays. Why the hell would I keep track of all my former buds, their wives, and their kids. Now dogs? I might keep track of your dog."

"Red died about four years ago. Remember that little female? Don't got a dog anymore. But I got two kids and another one on the way."

"Holy crap. You are a fertile motherfucker."

"No, she's the fertile one. I'm just the sperm donor, you know how it is."

Brady did.

"Casey's a nice girl. You'll like her. But you got to keep your hands off."

"That's alright, Riley. I've been healed. No more women for me. I just got Tate, my Doberman."

"Well, if you're still in Healdsburg, then we're only about an hour away. I'm up in Clearlake now, got a little piece of heaven. It's real quiet. We go out paddle boarding on the lake. It's a nice place to raise a family. You should try it sometime." Riley was funny with the jokes, but in-person, Brady would threaten to give him a punch on the chin.

"I'll be up in about two and a half hours. I'm going to bring my dog. I hope that's okay."

"I'll text you the address; you can do a GPS on it. But Tate's got to stay in the car. We got cats."

Shit.

RILEY'S PLACE WAS a typical lakeside cabin, added onto, probably as his family expanded, with tall pine trees to give the front and backyard good shade. He had a long dock extending from the back part of the property with two small rowboats tied off—one on the right and one on the left. From a couple of the trees, Riley had swung a hammock, family-sized, and it didn't take much imagination for Brady to see the scene of him, his wife, and their two kids all wrapped up in it. If Riley was still as active as he used to be, Brady bet there were some interesting moves the man would make. He'd probably got dumped a few times by the hammock until he got the hang of it.

It brought a smile to Brady's mouth. The first one in a while.

Chickens ran all over the place, chased by one nasty rooster who flattened the hens as he was mounting them, sending their beaks and necks to the dirt or sometimes the mud. As he walked with his buddy down toward the dock, the scrawny rooster headed right for Brady, who immediately knew what to do. He kicked the critter about ten feet into the air. The rooster landed on his feet, shook his head, and then found another hen to run after.

There was only one thing he hated more than cats. It was roosters, especially mean roosters.

Riley was still laughing when they sat down on a couple of Adirondack chairs with a small oak stump between them. His lady brought out a couple tall lemonades.

"You want something stronger, Brady?" she asked sweetly.

"No, it's the middle of the day, and I got to drive home. I need a DUI like a hole in the head."

"Suit yourself," she said as she sauntered back into the house. Her belly gave her hips an extra sway. Brady watched her and then noticed Riley was watching *him*.

"She's kind of nice, isn't she?" Riley whispered.

"She's fine. A regular baby maker."

"That she is. But babies make her happy, and I never had any until I met her so we just kind of go with the flow here. A couple extra mouths to feed, it's no big deal. I go hunting once a year, and we freeze most of it. We can fish a little bit in the lake. She's got a nice garden over there. You like a garden too. I heard you were doing some things like that. Little bit of green stuff, huh? Making some money at it?"

"No, not yet. I mean, I've had some ups and downs with it, but we're just getting started."

"*We're*? You got a partner?" Riley asked.

"I got Tate."

"Your dog."

"Hell yes, my dog! He's my partner. But yeah, I had plans, but I got something that's kind of come up, and I think it's going to ruin all that, at least for this season anyway."

Riley grabbed his lemonade, took a long sip, and then left his hands balanced on his knees. "So what's up?"

The lack of smile on his old buddy's face and a marked twinkle his eye showed Riley expected it would be something good to see his old friend after no contact for several years.

"You remember that dude Esquivel?" asked Brady.

"Well, he's a guy who's hard to forget, wouldn't you say?"

"That's a fact. Turns out, he's in California."

"How'd you find out about that?"

"I can't rightly say. I got a strange phone call from a rather official-sounding woman who told me that she had a job for me. And she was going to give me a lot of money to capture him."

"Dead or alive?" asked Riley.

"It's got to be alive, but she even told me we could carve him up some. I think accidents could happen. The main thing is I'd like to see this cretin off the street."

Riley studied him carefully, as if wondering whether he should bring a certain subject matter up. Instead, he nodded slowly. "You up to face all that, Brady?"

"I haven't thought of much else. I go to bed at night and hope to God I can dream. If I dream, it's all about Maggie." He hesitated to go further because the back of his throat was choking up, and again, he didn't want to show any form of weakness. But he'd just been talking to Tate and nobody else, so this conversation got to him a bit. He looked over at his truck. Tate was sitting in the driver's seat, his nose poking out of the rolled down window, staring right at him. He was watching guard over his master.

"And if it's a nightmare, it's Esquivel. Am I right?"

"Bingo." Brady began to relax.

"All right then. So you left off where she was going to pay you some money to go get this guy and turn him in… where?" Riley asked.

"We didn't quite get that far. But I do have some money in the bank, thanks to her. With the promise of more."

"How much more?"

"One million dollars, Riley. And I'd like to split it with you and anyone else we decide to hire. I can't do it alone. If you say no, of course I'll try. But it wouldn't be smart. I think we need five, six guys maybe?"

"Are you sure about this? I mean, is this legit, legal?"

"She says she has the capacity to make it go away— the kidnapping, that is. No one would have to serve any time for it. Not that that makes any difference to me. And the money's just gravy, but I could use it."

"Wow, that's a lot of money. But that's too much of a job for the two of us. I agree with you. We need about five guys at least."

"So are you in?" Brady asked his friend.

Riley's lady came out, bringing a plate of cookies. She laid them down on the stump, leaned over, gave Riley a kiss on the cheek, and then stood behind him, rubbing his shoulders. "The kids want you to come inside. They have something they want to show you." She briefly looked up at Brady and smiled, rather demure. Brady realized she was probably less than twenty-five years old.

"Just give me and Brady here about five, ten more minutes, and then I'll be in. Okay, sweetheart?"

"Brady, you're going to stay for supper?" she asked.

"No, I got to get back to Healdsburg before it gets too late. Tate's got a real funny stomach. If I don't feed him on time, he's irregular for the next week and a half. And I didn't bring any food with me, so I think we'll be headed home. But thanks for the invite. Maybe next time."

He was surprised that he even mentioned a next time. Things were changing in Brady's world.

As Riley watched her attractive rear end make its figure S's on the way to the back porch, it was Brady's turn to study his friend. "Riley, it's a big decision, and I know I'm asking a lot. I probably have no right to even ask you. You've got a nice life here. I'm not so sure if I was in your situation that I would trust an old fart like me who's more than likely going to get you into trouble."

Riley continued to stare at his lady until her frame disappeared behind the screen door. He looked directly into Brady's eyes. "Yeah, you are asking a whole lot more than you deserve. But fuck, wouldn't it be cool to nail that son of a bitch? If we can't kill him, maybe we could cut off one of his fingers and bury it in Maggie's grave. I'd do that with you. Hell, I'd cut off his foot and bury it there."

Brady stood up. "Nope. We're not going to desecrate her grave at all. But I got your meaning. So I guess I can count on you then?"

"You didn't even have to ask. Anything for you. And for Maggie."

CHAPTER 3

THE TWO FORMER teammates agreed that Riley should say his goodbyes at home and then head over to Brady's house to gear up and strategize. That way, he'd be out of earshot of the woman and children who probably would be worried if she heard what their plans were. Also, Riley would be less distracted. Brady hated for Riley to have to be re-reminded as the seconds and minutes ticked by of what he was going to be missing and perhaps risking, for the next few days.

But hopefully, they could wrap all this up in a week, if they got the right people to help them, and that's what they were going to discuss today.

Before Riley arrived, Brady checked his grows, repaired some camera angles and motion sensor lights that were working intermittently, and made sure that anybody who happened to come across his little patch would be met with a lot of scary stuff, like recordings of gunfire and sounds of growling alligators, coyotes, and bears. He even had a couple small explosive charges set up—not too over-the-top. He didn't want to make it sound like the whole mountain was going up in an explosion, which might attract local police and fire crews, or get complaints from the rural neighbors, who mostly tolerated Brady.

But everybody on the mountain knew he was eccentric as hell. Even when he came to town to get supplies, the good people of Healdsburg, who were used to tourists coming up from San Francisco and the Bay Area or places east, knew this particular mountain man, with his arms covered in tats, his hair usually uncombed and disappearing like the pelt of an old animal, and smelling like Tate—*this* guy was not to be messed with.

That was just fine with Brady.

He prepared some steaks to barbecue when Riley arrived and picked some zucchini and lettuce for a salad and some steamed vegetables. He got out some lean hamburger meat for Tate and mixed it with his kibbles, giving him an early supper.

"I don't want you begging for steak, Tate. Tonight, we got to be nice to our guest, okay?"

Tate dutifully looked up and then went right back to his eating.

Brady's phone signaled that somebody was at the bridge, so he sent the code to open the heavy steel gate and disarm his traps. In two minutes, Riley's old Jeep pickup truck came lumbering over the bridge and down the dirt road approach to his cabin. It was like déjà vu seeing him drive up like that, almost as if the last ten years had never happened. Those were the days before Maggie, when he'd just bought this place and planned to get out of the teams. He had reconsidered once Maggie came along and re-upped one last time. But during that period, she disappeared—kidnapped and murdered.

So Brady returned home alone.

In an odd sort of way, today things looked hopeful again, kind of like that time way back when. Before he'd lost her.

Tate stayed alert, standing by Brady's side, and waited until given the signal to go greet their guest. He didn't jump, but he licked and nuzzled Riley's knees and legs and thigh, nearly knocking his old friend over. Brady had forgotten about the finger that Riley lost on one of their missions. Riley told the whole team it was a good omen since it was the fourth finger on his left hand and meant he would never have to get married.

Of course, time changed all that.

"Bones, I thought I had paradise, but God almighty, this place is gorgeous. Green. And it's summertime."

"I've re-routed a few creeks. Not sure the Corps of

Engineers would like it. I've managed to dig a few wells. I'm almost off the grid except for electricity. I use propane, but everything I got here, I put together myself. It's like meditation, you know?"

"I totally get it." Riley said, eyeing the horizon. "I see your vegetables over there and grapes. You make your own wine?"

"Yep, and you're going to taste some tonight. It's not as good as it's going to be eventually, but I got time."

"I don't see any greenhouses. Where's your grow?"

"Down there a ways, out of sight, I can't fool the airplanes but managed to put a canopy over it. You want to see it tonight or you want to eat?"

"I'd rather eat, to be honest."

"You old pothead, Riley. She's really domesticated you, hasn't she?"

"Yeah, pretty much. You know, when you look into the eyes of a little person, half her and half me, it does something to you, Brady. I'm not going to lie. We faced some awful bad guys in our day, but it scares the shit out of me that I would ever disappoint one of those kids. I hope to God that Cassie never finds out how freaking scared I was when she delivered our first. I was so worried she wasn't going to make it, and the doctors finally had to haul me away. I missed the whole dang thing. Second time, I was a little smarter. But not much." He shook his head. "Kids, they do something to you. It's unbelievable, Brady."

Brady had been looking at his boots, making little designs with his toe. The subject matter was difficult for him to grasp. He decided to end it.

"Riley, you got to stop that. If we're going to do this, I don't want to hear anything more about your wife, your kids, the whole thing. I just don't want to hear it. It's not part of my life. It's not anything I'm ever going to have or do, and I just don't want to think about it. All I want to focus on is getting this monster picked up so he can't go hurt somebody else like he did my Maggie. And it makes it hard to sleep at night knowing that he's out there preying on other women and children. That's what I think about. I want to stop this guy. I want to make it so he's permanently off the map. If she'll let me, I'll put him away, too."

"It's not about the money at all, is it?"

"Not at all. I just want to get it done. As fast as possible, as efficiently as possible, nobody gets hurt except the bad guy. That's what we want. That's the goal and the mission."

The two friends turned around and headed toward the back door. Crossing their path were several chickens.

"So you got them too, right?" said Riley.

"Yep, I only keep the hens alive, though. When I

find out we got a chick that's a rooster, well, I cook it up and give it to Tate. Ain't that right, Tate?" he said as he patted the dog on his head.

"So how do you get babies then, if you have no roosters?" Riley asked.

"Well, about the time they start to crow, they can start having babies, right? They get a couple of days of fun. They start mounting my hens and get a few of them to lay fertile eggs. I separate those, and I hatch them. Then I let those grow up, and we have chicken for me and cooked rooster for old Tate here. But no, I don't have time for a mean old rooster like you got, Riley. That guy would not last on my farm. He'd either get a boot on his neck or blasted with my shotgun."

Riley chuckled. "Some things never change. You got to be in control all the time, don't you?"

"I can say that's an affirmative."

Laughing, they came inside. Brady fixed his simple dinner, and they sat talking about times past, some of the guys who didn't make it home, and some of the guys who did and what they were doing now. Brady had lost track of most of the men on his team, but he still remembered every man he failed over the years. He was careful not to tell anyone about that, though. Riley, on the other hand, was better at staying in touch.

"You're going to have to help me pick out some guys," Brady started. "I think we need a sharpshooter, a mechanic, a driver, and I'd like to get a backup medic, you know, just in case we run into something. I don't know if we'll find him in a warehouse full of damaged women or whether we'll find him on a back road somewhere, but it's possible we could even chase him all the way to Mexico. It would be good if we got somebody that spoke Spanish. I was thinking of Enemario Rodriguez for that job. And he's a hell of a shot too."

"Enemario would be a great choice," said Riley. "I like John Pawley for medic. You trained him yourself, I think, Brady."

"I did. He's a hell of a good guy. But I thought he was going to go to medical school."

"No, he couldn't make it. His grades were bad, and well, he kind of drifted off to doing some other things. He's doing carpentry now, building houses somewhere in Nevada. I'll bet he'd be interested, though. And he never had any money, remember that?"

"Oh yeah I remember that. He still owes me 40 bucks."

After a pause, Brady asked, "What about Carter Livingston for our driver, our mechanic, and general gadget guru? He could do some good stuff for us. I don't know exactly where we'll find Esquivel, and Carter's done some truck driving, too, so if we happen to find Esquivel in a big diesel rig, Carter could probably drive that puppy, don't you think?"

"Yeah, he's a solid guy. Got a family, though. He moved back to the South, but he's one I would go after. I got a friend who knows him. I'll reach out, if you want, after dinner and see if we can locate him."

"I know Enemario lives down in San Diego. That's where most of his family is. I've got his number, but I don't have John Pawley's."

"I have you covered," said Riley.

After several phone calls, the three gentlemen they were hoping to get were finally onboard. It was going to take a few days for the team to assemble, so Riley and Brady decided to do some surveillance of the area where Rojas had been sighted near the Fresno area, a small sleepy town called Selma, California. They decided to bring Tate along. The rest of the men were going to show up within the week. Plus, Brady wanted at least a day to plan their operation. But first, he needed to see what they were dealing with.

"You going to take Tate on the real mission?" asked Riley.

"I don't think so. You suppose your Cassie could look out for him for me?"

"Does he like kids?"

"I think so. I mean, if I talk to him a little bit, he'd be fine. It's just that he's never been around kids. He'll chase anything that runs, and with your guys so small, you're going to have to keep the kids away when they are playing. But I think he'd be all right. I know he'd be fine with Cassie. The one thing I'm concerned about is your cats. And that rooster. He may not make it if Tate's there."

"Well, that's going to be on Tate's conscience now, isn't it? That'll be between him and his maker."

They both chuckled at Riley's comment.

Tate sat in the second seat of Brady's four-door king cab, stoically listening to their conversation. He had given up his normal perch, which was up front next to Brady. Today, that seat was taken by Riley.

They had left early in the morning, but by the time they reached the Central Valley, it was beginning to get dark and was near suppertime. They located a small motel that wouldn't set them back too much, next to a Mexican restaurant. Brady made Tate's food and left him in the motel room while they went next door for their dinner.

The small restaurant had a wonderful smell as soon as they walked in. A real mom-and-pop operation with homemade tamales, tortillas being cooked right in front of them on a big iron slab, and grilled fresh vegetables. Brady was in heaven. They passed on the margaritas and decided to each have one beer, remarking to the other how drastically things had changed.

"Riley, you're—what?—thirty-eight? Thirty-nine?"

"Yep, I'm thirty-eight. Same as you."

"Nope, I'll be forty next year. I'm thirty-nine, one whole year older."

"Well, Bones, I always knew you were an old man. You just keep getting better and better. Me? I'm going to stop aging next year. Or when I hit forty. That's the last birthday I'll ever have."

The comment was odd because they were going to be in danger's way soon. But he cleared his mind of any ill thoughts and decided to focus on the mission at hand.

"In the morning, I'd like to start asking some questions, carefully, see if we get any vibes as far as people who have noticed young girls missing. I've got some pictures I cut out of a couple of magazines we can be asking around about like we're relatives or something."

"That sounds good. Good cover anyway."

"But tonight, I'd like to head over to the ranch. I had a name of El Padre Negro. I think that means the Black Priest Ranch. Do you know anything about it?" asked Brady.

"No. Never heard of it. But I'll bet somebody in town has. We'll find it."

They walked through several bars in the outskirts on their way back to the motel, stopping to pretend to drink a beer but mostly trying to gather information. They showed the pictures around, sometimes going together, sometimes going separately, and eventually found a young Hispanic waitress who knew where the ranch was located. She gave instructions in part English and part Spanish, but Riley was able to cobble together enough of an instruction so they could head in that direction.

They came upon a compound bordered by chain link fence with razor wire on top, which to Brady was a dead giveaway. In the distance, lights shined on one long metal warehouse with its doors open, revealing several large vehicles inside, including a camper and a school bus. Nearby, several shipping containers were parked along with trucks and large farm equipment. A ranch style home sat in the middle of the compound, surrounded by large trees. It didn't take them long to notice that the grounds were patrolled with men carrying automatic weapons.

"Are you feeling what I'm feeling?" asked Brady.

"Hell yes. I'm going to recommend that we get some drones, and we get some eyes on these folks. We're going to have to watch the comings and goings, log that in. But you and I out here, we're too exposed. We need more numbers. Don't you think?" Riley answered.

"Yep. My thoughts exactly."

Brady created a rough sketch of the layout of the compound. They were able to pace off two of the sides and estimated the whole area was roughly five acres. A small orchard to one side had seen better days. A filbert or walnut orchard of some kind and citrus trees were closer to the house. They noticed a large cornfield and several coops containing fowl, mostly chickens but other species as well. The whole compound was not very tidy, with broken pieces of equipment and vehicles allowed to rust in the hot sun of the Central Valley. Unlike some of the orchards and farms in the Fresno area, this one had fallen on hard times. But it did contain a large warehouse and have shipping containers, which was something they were particularly interested in, since it could transport their human trafficking cargo.

Back at the motel, they retired for the evening and planned to return North to meet the rest of their crew.

In the morning, Brady struck up a conversation with the desk clerk.

"Have you ever heard of a gentleman who lives down here named Esquivel Rojas?"

The young man was obviously affected by the name but shook his head mutely.

"How about your folks? You have more family staying here?"

"¡Sí! My family lives here. My grandfather owns this motel, and my parents run the restaurant next door. But I do not know this man."

The young clerk appeared to be about twenty years of age with a light dusting of facial hair, barely out of high school. His eyes shifted from side to side as he spoke, giving Brady the distinct impression he was lying through his teeth.

"So the ranch in Selma, the Padre Negro, we understand this man owns the ranch?" asked Riley.

"I don't know who owns the *rancho*, but they are from Mexico. I believe the owners have a nice house downtown in Fresno, in the Pruneyard area?"

"That's a nice older neighborhood in Fresno, big houses, very expensive," Riley said, nodding his head to Brady and the young man, who also indicated he agreed.

"Okay, thank you." Brady handed the young man twenty dollars, and the boy pushed it back in Brady's direction.

"No, Señor, I am just trying to be hospitable. I don't know much about anything about the ranch, except that I have heard my parents talk about the owner living sometimes in that neighborhood. He never comes here. You will never see him here or at the restaurant. That's my understanding anyway."

Realizing he had probably said too much, the boy excused himself and left the desk unattended. Brady turned to Riley.

"We'll do a little scouting, and then let's head

north. That suit you?"

"I can't wait to get out of here." Riley was the first to exit the door. Brady retrieved Tate from their room, left the keys inside, and loaded their gear. The three of them drove off.

CHAPTER 4

THE SHORT TRIP Brady and Riley made from Selma to Fresno was highlighted with increasing numbers of warehouses and business signs the closer they got to Fresno. The rural feel of the small Central Valley town was completely erased as they entered the outskirts of Fresno proper.

"You ever been to Yosemite, Riley?" Brady asked as they passed the signs to Mariposa.

"Yes, once when I was, oh, about six, I guess. Again later on, before I joined the Navy. Beautiful place. You remember those Firefalls?"

"I sure do. Boy, my folks loved taking us there. They don't do it any longer, but there was some talk of them doing a modified Firefall. Was sure pretty."

"Yeah, just one of those things where we didn't know any better. Probably wasn't very good for the environment. Just like my dad used to talk about those x-ray machines in shoe stores. Remember those? You put your foot in there, and you could see your bones. And then some of the employees wound up getting radiation sickness from exposure to it. My mom worked for a radiologist who was all shriveled up—wrinkled—and his spine and his knuckles were swollen. He had radiation poisoning. They never used to put lead doors on their x-ray rooms. He used to dictate his reports right outside the room. Got a full dose every single day. And he died young too."

"That's a shame."

Brady didn't much care for this part of California. He much preferred the lush, green areas in Sonoma County and farther north. He didn't want to tell Riley this, but he didn't even like Lake County, either, except for the parts around the lake. He was more a Florida or Kansas or Northern California type of guy, someplace where they'd leave him alone with lots of green, fertile land and space. And in Florida, well, you had to pretty much hang out with the alligators to get that. But he liked the people, he liked the colors, and he loved the long stretches of beach with thousands of places to dip a boat in the Bay or the ocean and have a great time fishing.

He realized every place was not perfect. That's why living in Healdsburg made a lot of sense. Most people didn't even know it existed, unless they were foodies or wine connoisseurs. He didn't mind that. And he wasn't living there for those things anyway.

They turned off the freeway and headed toward the Pruneyard section, but first, they needed some breakfast to tide them over. They found a mom-and-pop diner advertising fresh homemade pies and biscuits, and Brady couldn't resist.

Their waitress was friendly and agreed to help them find Esquivel, saying she knew about him by reputation, that he was a good man, helping kids in school. She described the house where he lived, indicating it was a rust-colored property with red tile roof and a large blue fountain in the front courtyard. It had black gates, and on the front of the gates was a dragon design.

"El Dragon," she called him.

"Not Padre Negro?" Brady asked.

"No. El Dragon. He breathes fire." Then the waitress clammed up as someone walked inside and sat at the counter in front of her. Brady didn't want to look for fear of getting her in trouble. But he had a feeling that whomever sat to his right was someone he should probably follow.

Riley didn't have the same problem so leaned across and examined Brady's neighbor. As he got close to whisper something, Brady stopped him.

"Riley, not now. Let's talk outside," Brady said, half whispering.

"Suits me fine. You done?"

"Yeah. Done as I'm going to be."

On the way out, he noticed the tanned and dark-haired Mexican cowboy with a white hat, hand-tooled boots, matching belt, and a clean blue and white checked long sleeve button-down shirt slowly stirring his coffee. He was not a ranch hand and could have been a wealthy rancher himself. But something gave Brady pause.

Outside, Brady handed Tate a sausage patty he'd picked up before they left the restaurant, but he cautioned the dog. "Tate, I'm sorry. I know you want it, but don't eat it if it's going to turn your stomach."

As Riley stepped up into the cab, he muttered, "Man, you treat that dog like, well, your son."

Brady growled.

Riley shrugged and looked out the window to his right. "Just saying, you don't have to be so touchy. You know it's not a bad thing that you love your dog."

"I told you not to talk about kids or women."

"How the hell are we not going to talk about kids or women when we're going after a guy who steals kids and women? I mean, that's just not going to happen, Brady. You're going about this all wrong." Riley sighed and crossed his arms, leaning back in the squeaky seat. "You have this concrete wall built up like the steel fence on your goddamn bridge. And you wear your emotions on your sleeve. Everyone knows how you feel about it. You don't have to keep reminding me. I'm not talking about your situation. I'm talking about your love for your *dog,* man. And that has nothing to do with whether or not you have a woman or kids." He tightened his crossed arms and waited for a response.

Brady was going to explode with something terse and dangerous but decided against it. He sucked it up and went another direction.

"I apologize, my friend." The words nearly stuck in his throat. "Your point is well-taken. But you have a score to settle with Tate."

In the rear-view mirror, Brady eyed Tate sitting in the second seat, tall and menacing as he always looked, and smiled at the dog. Riley also turned and, after taking a long glance at the drooling Doberman, turned back facing front very slowly. "He does influence people. I'd say that dog understands English all too well."

"Well, he ought to. I talk to him every day. He is the only person I talk to ever."

After a short pause, Riley continued. "Okay. I'm sorry. Is that acceptable?"

"Yes, and just like I said, I am too."

Brady knew that would be the end of it. The discussion was hammered out just like an old piece of meat. Neither one of them was going to carry a grudge, and that was the beauty of having deep and thorough conversations with another team guy. You didn't have to use as many words. You could just growl, grunt, and fart or something, and the guy would just know. Unlike the female population or children, who did whatever the hell they felt like doing all the time and messed with your insides at the drop of a hat. Brady liked hanging around Riley for this very fact. It was simple. There was no question they were loyal to each other, and it was relaxing.

Around women and children, he could never relax.

Brady was just about to turn the key when they observed the Latino cowboy exit the restaurant and jump into a brand-new heavy duty four-door Ford pickup. The truck had dark tinted windows such that it was impossible to even see the driver's expression.

"You know those things cost nearly $100,000 now? Can you believe that, Brady?" Riley pointed out.

"Yeah, because of all the gadgets, the electronics, and stuff. I guess they're having a hard time getting those parts from overseas. That probably means this thing I'm driving is worth two-thirds that. Heck, that's almost double what I paid for it."

"Unbelievable." Riley shook his head. Brady started the engine and followed the Ford truck until it turned to the right, which was the opposite direction they were going. He stopped at the crosswalk. "Do we go left or right, Riley?"

"I say follow your hunch, Brady. Let's follow this guy, but don't let him onto us. Pretend like you're checking on an address or something, and so you can go slow and stop and start."

"Roger that."

The truck pulled into a convenience strip mall consisting of a beauty store, a liquor store, a nail salon, and a massage parlor. He parked his car in front of the liquor store but walked into the nail salon.

"Now you don't see that every day. A Latino cowboy going in to get his nails and toes done. Why, those boots are going to wreck anything—"

Just then, the cowboy reappeared from the door and looked straight at them, as he chewed on a toothpick.

"Fuck," mumbled Brady. "We're going to have to move on."

"No shit." Riley made a point to nod to the other side of the street using his forehead to indicate something Brady should look at. But he did it just to deflect whatever interest the cowboy had in the two of them.

It was obvious they'd been made.

After Brady took the turn, he doubled back and headed in the opposite direction so they could find the home Mr. Esquivel lived in. It didn't take long before the dusty brown fields and warehouse districts turned yet again. This time it was lush 100-year-old trees, well-manicured lawns, and tremendous estates behind tall fences.

One by one, they passed mansions built on several acres, practically larger than their team 5 building on Coronado, in a subdivision with streets wider than most freeways. Brady liked the area, and in the hot weather, the lush foliage and tall shady trees were very attractive. The whole neighborhood seemed pleasant and peaceful. It was hard to imagine that a sex trafficker and murderer would be living in one of these homes.

They slowly drove up and down several streets until they found the unmistakable rust-colored home with the shiny black gates in front, inlaid with a crest in the outline of a dragon, fire and all, in the center of each side. The concrete walls surrounding the home made viewing the activity inside impossible. But they did see an armed guard off to the right. They also saw two other men having a cigarette in the opposite corner, long guns strapped across their shoulders. Their white cowboy hats obscured their faces in shadow.

Brady made a note of the address and called it out to Riley, who wrote it down in his notebook. They drove around the block, which was how big the property was—one huge city block. A rear entrance in the back had a sliding steel door, like Brady had seen in

South America and parts of Mexico.

It was clearly a fortress, designed to protect the occupants from any nosey neighbors or hapless salesman. Even though it was a ranch-style home, the sprawling design contained an upper level off to the right side with a balcony all around it. It was a perfect vantage point to survey the flat landscape and the houses and neighborhood nearby. The balcony appeared empty.

The ground floor was larger than the upper wing and appeared to have multiple bedrooms and probably a private interior courtyard. Several huge palm trees grew right from the center of the house. Brady figured it was a small patio where whoever was there could be totally protected from everything but the air.

"We're going to get some drones. We need to take a closer look. If we're lucky, we might catch some sightings of Mr. Rojas, don't you, Riley?"

"I think you'd be right. Only two ways in, quiet neighborhood, easy to get out if you had to in a hurry. You could tear down this road at sixty to seventy miles an hour and probably never see a soul. During the hot weather, I'll bet everybody just stays inside with air conditioning. But if you had to get out of Dodge, you could do it here."

"Meaning him or us?" asked Brady.

"Either one." Riley shrugged again and took out a small pair of binoculars he had tucked into his shirt pocket, examining the trees inside the concrete perimeter wall.

"I'm seeing some cameras, a lot of wiring going on, and looks like they got a basket or two up there. Yeah, I see a ladder and a little guardhouse inside one of those palm trees. See that cluster over to the right? They got a little observation tower there. I bet at night he goes infrared."

"Wouldn't surprise me. So we got to be ready for that then," added Brady. "Let's shoot some pictures and get out of Dodge."

As they drove home, the two SEAL buddies made lists of things they were going to need. Mostly, they needed night vision equipment, some explosive devices, knives, some equipment for close contact hand-to-hand-style combat, some zip ties, and sidearms. Brady indicated that they'd have to try to find a rooftop somewhere so they could be covered. He didn't want to break in if they had a sighting of Rojas without protection from cover fire, if needed.

Riley said he noticed several second-story additions on homes that might work, and he made a note to scout those out on their next trip.

"When do you think we'll bring everybody back down here?" Riley asked.

"I'm thinking two days, maybe three?" Brady

turned to face Riley. "Sort of depends on when everybody arrives. I'm hoping they'll get to Sonoma County today or tomorrow at the latest. Gives us a day to gear up and strategize. We'll draw out both locales, and then we'll toss it around. I want everybody's eyes on this before we do anything. This isn't going to be my op. I need everybody's input. And I don't want to make a focused plan without it."

"Music to my ears. We can do it."

When they returned to Healdsburg, Riley got out his computer. He'd been tasked with running property searches and wanted to research owners' names of both properties. The house was registered to a corporation called Dragon Limited.

"I got your dragon, Brady."

Brady joined him at the table. Looking down at the screen, he whistled. "So there he is, huh?"

Riley had researched the name, and the county records showed a nonprofit organization using the address of the house as its office. It was a center for orphaned and exploited children. A smiling picture of Esquivel Rojas himself was plastered in the middle of a Fresno Bee newspaper article about his foundation, *Angelfind.*

"Can you believe the nuts on this guy? Here he goes and steals kids and women, sells them into sex slavery, and then opens up an orphanage, for Chrissake?"

"My guess is he doesn't think he'll get caught. Wonder why he thinks that?" mused Brady.

"Yeah, that's odd, isn't it? Most those guys, they hide in the hills. This guy's right out in plain sight. I mean it doesn't take long to find him. We found him right away, and we didn't even do much of a record search. He's just right there," stated Riley, pointing to his computer screen.

"Maybe somebody else is protecting him. Do you suppose that could be?" Brady asked.

"It sure would be a whole lot better if your gal on the phone would give us some background. Can you reach her?"

"Haven't tried. Something tells me it'll go to a non-working number or disconnect or something. I'm sure her phone is scrambled. No, we're on our own."

"Well, hell's bells, as long as the money keeps flowing, I guess we just forge along, right?" Riley asked.

"I can't say as I like it that way. That's why I want to make sure we know what we're doing. I don't want to go kick a hornet's nest over, spook the guy, and then have him hightail it back to Mexico."

Riley looked up at him. "Do we have authority to go to Mexico?"

"We have the authority to get him wherever he is in

the globe. It's just that it'll be a lot easier in California."

But Brady was already worried that might not be a true statement.

CHAPTER 5

THE FIRST NEW team member to arrive was John Pawley. John had been one of the best junior medics Brady ever trained, a natural-born healer with good hands and quick wit. It was helpful to have someone who didn't panic in an emergency, someone who could identify the problem, quickly mitigate possible further injury, and thereby probably save someone's life. He also was a skilled surgeon, if quick battlefield amputations and wound stitching could be called surgery. It was more like butchering, Brady thought to himself.

John had gotten in trouble with some pain killers and his attention span difficulties. He'd had to bail out of the pre-medical courses he was required to take before he could apply to medical school. He washed out and joined his then father-in-law building houses around the Las Vegas area.

His hair was a little long, sporting a four-inch ponytail, but other than that, he was clean-shaven, his eyes were clear, and he didn't look like he had any shakes, reddening skin, or indications of substance abuse. And that was the first question Brady had asked him on the phone.

"John, my man, you look fit. Tanned. How's married life?"

Brady didn't really want to know how his married life was, but it was something he had to get out of the way, because he knew someone coming from a recent divorce would have to be watched over extra special, especially if he had a new proximity to drugs and alcohol. John would be carrying a lot of tempting designer drugs on their mission, while Brady was busy doing the prep work, running the mission, and manning the comms.

"Always a puppy dog with your questions," John answered with a sly grin. "As a matter of fact, my blood pressure is impeccable, and my hands perfect, except for a few scars from the hammering and stuff. I haven't touched a drop of alcohol or Oxy in over five years. I've been divorced for four, so I had a stretch there where I was tempted, but I'm good now. Got a new girlfriend, and life's good. I'm finally making some money. 'Bout ready to pay off my last debt." He grinned again, showing his pearly whites.

"I see you got your teeth done, too."

"That I did, with my first big paycheck," he said, showing them off again.

Brady always thought he could've been an actor with his rugged good looks. He never knew John to have trouble with the ladies but, like himself and several others on the team, definitely had trouble keeping them. And it had nothing at all to do with satisfaction. It was from the lack of attention. John probably was less so.

"John, I'm glad to hear it. I didn't question when you told me you were clean. Just had to ask. Part of the job."

"I got you, Chief. I know."

John grabbed Riley, and they gave a manly hug, something John didn't do with Brady.

"Glad to have you, John." Then Riley grabbed the carpenter by his upper arms, feeling his muscles. "Well, you'd never get those working in a hospital. I'd say building houses has been good for you, bud."

"Vegas isn't exactly a family town, but I make good money. And people are moving there in droves. Not exactly where I'd like to settle down someday, but for right now, with the shows, the pretty girls, all the glitz and movie stars, and a chance to make some money, it's my kind of excitement."

Brady began his host duties by taking the newcomer's duty bag and bringing it inside the house. "We're going to bunk in here for a night or two, until every-body comes. We got two more on the way. I'm going to have to put you up on the couch here, unless you'd rather be on the floor. I got extra blankets and pillows no problem. The head's in there. I got another one outside off the back porch. Help yourself to anything in the refrigerator, and if you've got any special needs as far as food requests or anything, I'm not listening. Mostly what I feed people is wild game, beef, and vegetables because I got it all here. And if you tell me you don't eat pork, well, you're going to be the sorriest son of a gun you've ever seen."

Brady was having fun.

"You raise pigs?" asked John.

"In a way. We got wild boar up in these hills. Can you believe it?"

"I understand they're mighty tasty."

Riley had been fidgeting. "So while you guys are exchanging recipes and talking about menu plans, I'm getting back on the computer. Brady and I are re-searching the area we're going to be heading to as soon as the rest of the team arrives. I got more stuff to do and maybe some calls before we can formally show you what we got. So excuse me."

Riley left the living room, walked into the dining room, and took up his seat across from his computer.

"Okay, John, I'm going to give you a medic kit that

I made up. I'm going to take the pony pack while you take the heavy. I got the radios and other stuff. You'll be the lead medic on this team, and hopefully, we won't need it. We might find women and children there, so we need to take note and plan accordingly. They also might get hurt in the crossfire while we're getting this guy, or they could be in rough shape, abused. We don't know what we'll find, but we have to be prepared for all of it." Brady studied John as he finished. "I need you to ask me questions, because I got a lot going on, and I may not remember to tell you everything."

"I get who this guy is. I know the history, and by the way, I'm sorry, Brady. So sorry."

Brady held up his hand as a stop sign. "Not necessary, but I appreciate it."

"My understanding is we're supposed to nab him, not take him out. Is that right?"

"You would be correct. Yes, sir."

John scratched the back of his head. "And what about the other guys? He's going to have bodyguards and handlers. Are we authorized to use lethal force?"

"My understanding is that we can, but we probably shouldn't. There is a chance that we'll be dealing with some Mexican nationals, and Rojas himself is not a U.S. citizen. At least I don't think he is. He wasn't a few years ago. That's just not the information I have anyway. So we have to be careful about handling people from other countries here, but my understanding is any of our actions will be protected from scrutiny."

"Just who are we working for?" John asked.

"I'm not quite sure." Brady was going to be honest with everybody on the team. "My guess is, this guy was being protected or is being protected by someone in our government, and we are either working for a private outfit or another branch of the government that needs to bring him in. I honestly don't know whether they're going to try him or just get him out of the way, because he is pulling off some bad stuff. Everyone knows it. He has been doing it for more than a decade now. And we just found out he also has set up a nonprofit organization, finding homes for orphan children. Isn't that sweet?"

"Wow. That's a new one."

"And that's what I'm checking on," shouted Riley from across the room. "I've got a bunch of names to research here. This guy is a registered charity. He actually can take cash donations."

"Well, that's a perfect money laundering scheme, if you ask me," said John.

"Exactly."

"Any other questions?" Brady asked again.

"How are you assured that we're protected, like if

someone were to get shot and die? We're not going to do it intentionally, but things happen, right?"

"It depends on the mission. You know, John, if it's going to save one of you guys, one of us, no question. I will use lethal force. If Esquivel's going to kill a kid or a woman, I'm going to injure him, but I'll kill his buddies. As long as what we do can be justified, I think they'll play ball with us. It sounds like they've got more power that I'll ever have. And I asked a bunch of times, and I never got any answers really. All she said—"

"She?"

"Yes, the nice lady on the phone who hired me, us, said that they'll cover and make sure that anything we do is buried. We won't be tried or convicted or have to worry about consequences. That said, we go in and slaughter everybody, we'll be in trouble. Let's just say they're playing ball with us, and as long as the money keeps coming and it's something we can do, then we do it. If it requires we do something we can't do, then we back away."

John looked down at his feet.

"That enough for you?" Brady asked.

"With two hundred thousand dollars for a week's work?"

"I'm hoping, yes."

"Hell yeah, I'm in. When you think about it, we never really were protected anyway. I mean, if the bad guys didn't get us and we got out of line, the Navy has a way of pretty much ruining your life. And they've done it to some of our team guys, so I always had a healthy skepticism during the time we served together. I mean, in this world today, how the Hell do we know who's telling the truth and who isn't?"

"That's exactly what I thought, John. And there's only one reason in the world I would take this kind of risk, and that's to get Mr. Rojas away from as many women and children in the future as possible. That's what we did when we were on the teams; that's what we'll do now. We'll be a force for good. At least that's what I'm telling myself. But you must make your own peace with this. And if you're not comfortable, John, you can go. Honest to God." Brady showed him his open palms and waited for John to respond.

"I'm all-in, Chief. You've got my eyes and ears, my hands, my guts, my heart. I'm actually excited about this."

Brady could've just grabbed the guy and given him a big bear hug, but that wasn't going to be how he would lead this team. He just experienced the satisfaction of having a good man aligned with him. He knew he could count on him. And he was excited about the prospects himself.

But he never wanted to show it.

Enemario Rodriguez was the second team member

to arrive. Raised on the border between California and Mexico, the son of immigrant parents, he was immersed in the rich tradition of early California, the Spanish, and the Mexican Free State. He had a grandfather who rode with Pancho Villa. He also had relatives who lived in Texas, and those Tejanos fought on both sides of several wars, including several Indian wars. In fact, except for his parents who were sharecroppers and farmers, valued employees of several large farms in the Escondido and San Diego areas, most of the rest of his family were warriors.

He'd been comfortable with guns ever since he shot his first squirrel at four years old, stealing his father's pistol. It was a story he liked to tell on cold snowy nights in Afghanistan as the team was huddled waiting for further orders. He was a former Marine who decided, after passing up a lucrative opportunity to work for Border Patrol or Homeland Security, to stay out of the political fray. He had joined the San Diego Police Force, where he served with distinction.

Of course, politics became a larger and larger subject for not only the police forces and first responders but now the military. Several years ago, after he put in his five, he decided it was time to get out of the police and sniper warrior world and start becoming a regular Joe. The task was impossible. He missed the action most of all.

But one thing bothered him more than anything else. He was never able to have an impact on some of the things that affected his family the most.

Human trafficking.

He had cousins, friends of cousins, friends of relatives on both sides of the border in Texas, New Mexico, Arizona and California—all victims in one form or another of the human sex trafficking trade. Young girls in his family went missing in a larger proportion than many of his Caucasian brothers in the Marines. Most of his SEAL friends didn't experience firsthand the heartache and trauma he and his family did. It was a difficult subject to discuss and even more difficult to track and try to right some of the wrongs. That haunted him.

Brady had a lot of confidence in the man, and he came highly recommended by Riley, who was about the best judge of character on the planet.

Enemario stood at the gate when Brady buzzed him in. He climbed back inside his huge Hummer, a vehicle he had turned into a stretched machine two feet longer than the average Suburban. It had every kind of bell and whistle anyone would ever want, including surveillance cameras, a satellite dish buried in the top, solar panels he could use to charge up any electronic devices inside, and other gadgets he was legendary for creating. He also was the very best drone maker there was, especially coming up with models that were able to drop little incendiary or explosive devices on unsuspecting bad guys very quietly and without warning.

Brady figured him an integral part of this mission since so many of the girls they would be dealing with were Spanish speaking. They needed to have insight into that community and all the languages and dialects they might run across.

Enemario's huge vehicle sounded like a semi-truck coming down the driveway. Brady, Riley, and John looked in awe as their new team member arrived.

The large green monster painted in silver fleck came to a screeching halt, dust and rocks flying in every direction as if it was a landed helicopter. When the dust settled and the engine roar ended, the door opened and out jumped five-foot-four Enemario Rodriguez, in full body armor.

The only thing not military issue were his cowboy boots, pure snakeskin and intricately tooled with colorful patterns around the toe, the heel, and extending up the front of his shin.

"*Buenos dias, amigos!*" Enemario was a character in a Marvel comic book series, or so it seemed to Brady.

"Welcome to the Wild Pig Ranch. You here to learn how to ride horses or meet pretty women?" Brady shouted to him. He was still swishing the dust out of his eyes with his hand.

"Ah, yes. I like those fillies. Both kinds. I don't know if I could ride one today, since I have my woman back home. Plus, I have put on a little bit of weight." He held his tummy, which was completely flat and didn't show an ounce of flab anywhere.

"You fucking liar," said Riley.

The two friends hugged each other quickly and then released arms.

John stepped forward and extended his hand. He had never met Enemario before. "Pleasure to meet you."

Enemario graciously shook his hand, squinting and showing a gold tooth, his upper-right canine. If he wore golden earrings, a patch, and a red bandana, he could have easily passed for a pirate.

"I hear you got this gig going. I'm going crazy coaching my nephew's soccer team, driving my mother to doctors' appointments, and trying to find work that doesn't make me feel like a schoolboy. You under-stand?" Enemario held his arms out to the sides.

Every single one of the team nodded their heads. They'd all been there too.

"Bring your gear inside, anything that's not safe out here in the beast. Geez, how the hell did you have something like that made?"

"Oh, this old thing?" Enemario said, pointing to his monster truck. "I had so many favors owed to me, and there are several body shops in Tijuana that used to help me when I was on the force in San Diego. We were a source of information for each other. I did as much to help those guys as I did people in California. I got this done for practically nothing. The only thing I had to do was to pay for the stretching and the frame-work. They don't do that in Mexico. They bring that somewhere else. But I got it done. It rides like hell, like a semi would, but it sure does impress everybody who sees it."

Brady realized it would be a little too conspicuous for them if Enemario brought this vehicle. He wasn't so sure the man's pride and joy was going to be able to be used. But Brady kept his mind open to it anyway. "So rig it up, bring your stuff inside, and let me show you where you can sleep, okay?"

Enemario waddled like the Michelin Man, huge bulging shoulders and hands that hung nearly to his short knees. The size of his upper torso did not match his lower torso, even though his legs were fully muscular. He would have made one hell of a wrestler, Brady thought.

The man pulled out a duty bag that probably weighed more than one hundred pounds, which told Brady he probably brought lots of gadgets and gear to show them. He followed the rest of them inside the house.

"Would you look at this?" Enemario said, searching the interior. "If I didn't know better, I'd figure this was designed by a woman. This is not you, my friend."

Both Riley and John shook their heads. John swore and turned around so he wouldn't have to show Brady his features. Brady knew he was expected to growl, but he decided to just let Enemario have it straight, right in the solar plexus, but with words not his fist.

"As they all now know, I lived here for a time before I met—" He hesitated, because that little catch in the back of his throat popped up again. He coughed and apologized. "I'm not going to lie, Enemario. I talk to Maggie in my dreams. I see her here. You can say what you want, and I don't give a damn, but her hand is in this house. I tried to make it a place she would want to come, and my sister reads all that shit about angels and vampires and crap, so maybe one of those characters will resurrect her, and she can come back as a ghost. I'd take her anyway I could. But no, this was all my doing. I sold the house in San Diego after she was gone."

It was an awkward pause. A very awkward pause. Brady could see Enemario felt horrible about the communication.

"I'm sorry, man. Riley told me, and I didn't think."

"I'm used to it, but don't do it again."

And that was the thing—the thing about them all,

Brady thought to himself. Being in the company of other warriors, other men, they understood things had to be left private. You had to trust your buddies enough to tell them the crap going on in your life, not to complain just so they'd know what you're dealing with. Not every detail, of course, but you'd have to tell them, or they'd think you were batshit crazy. And even if you were, it was the right thing to do. Then after they knew they had stepped onto hallowed ground and had to wipe their feet off, they'd be on their best behavior.

That's all there was too it. Simple plan, and everybody got along. And that's how they were going to have to charge into battle.

Together.

That's the way it always was, and that's the way it always would be.

Even with all the warts and lumps of this little group, Brady finally felt he'd met his true family.

CHAPTER 6

CARTER LIVINGSTON DROVE up in a brand-new Mercedes. He'd been a team guy for nearly fifteen years before he invented a piece of body armor and sold it to a large defense contractor for nearly two billion dollars. Born and raised in Mississippi, Carter had grown up repairing tractors and working on his family's modest farm, but he was compelled to join the Special Forces and become a Navy Seal while watching the videos of the 9/11 terrorist attack. He just could not sit home, plow fields, and pretend it didn't happen. Even though he didn't know anyone in the Twin Towers that day, he had been outraged with the destruction, death, and turmoil it caused the entire New York area, the country, and the whole world.

Without a college education, his prospects were slim, since he didn't have technical skill that could land him an important job, other than a farmhand. But he was one of the best mechanics that Brady had ever seen. He could fix anything. In fact, he could make anything and, just like Enemario, knew a lot about drone making.

The first thing Carter had done when he received the money from his invention was pay off the family farm. Then he helped his parents buy a few thousand acres beside it. Having gotten his family on their feet, he took his time and found several charities he donated anonymously to, with strict rules for how the charity operated and who the charity benefitted. He'd seen his share of organizations that only served those who ran the charities and wasn't interested in supporting those selfish endeavors.

The Navy had been good to him, and even after he knew he was going to be coming into a fortune, he continued with the Teams until his enlistment was over.

Although it had been rumored he was a great connoisseur and lover of women, he had a secret that he guarded very safely. With his money, he could now do anything he wanted for the rest of his life. So when he got the call to right this one wrong he knew Brady wanted to take care of, he was all-in. In short, he missed putting his life on the line for important causes. And there wasn't anything he hated more than somebody who enslaved women and children for their own gain.

The 6'4" handsome and extremely gentlemanly former warrior exited his Mercedes wearing a business suit and carrying an attaché case.

Brady didn't know how to react. The last time he'd seen Carter was when they were knee deep in dust, trying to evacuate villagers who had been attacked after the team had gone through and cleared out several top gorilla leaders. He and Carter had walked the streets as the bodies of young children and women swung from several government building eaves in the hot sun. It was a scene straight out of hell.

Carter and Brady never had more than a few words to say to each other during their time on the Teams together, but it wasn't their words that spoke. It was the actions they took that said everything they needed each other to know. If a radio was broken, Carter would fix it. If more supplies were needed, he knew where to go and find it. He could blend in any crowd. He spoke seven different languages, and he had an extreme hatred for bullies and people who threw their weight around, especially upper-level military, desk jockeys who put them in harm's way without properly evaluating the real risks of the missions.

Carter had a tough time with their commanding officer, Lieutenant Roland Stanley, who outranked everyone, including Chief Rogers. Stanley made it very plain he wanted Carter out of the military, off of his

Seal team, and accused him of making mistakes and being lazy on the job. The truth was Carter was never one to lick anybody's boots. And Roland Stanley had a hair trigger, an emotional problem stemming from his insecurity as an officer. He constantly complained about not getting the respect he felt he was owed. The whole team knew he'd throw any of them under the bus just to prove he was more powerful.

He had been a selfish, dangerous man who had grown up being handed all his opportunities, rather than earning them. To Stanley, Carter had been a threat to his authority.

Several months before Carter left the Teams, Stanley put Carter up on charges. Everyone knew they were bullshit. Chief Rogers came to bat for Carter and got the upper management to back off. The men in their platoon at SEAL Team 5 never trusted Stanley again. Carter and Brady formed a bond as a result that was still remembered today, and always would be. That act of common decency would always be remembered deep in Carter's heart.

"I'm wondering what the hell you're doing here, Carter, but I am very glad you came," said Brady to his new teammate.

The two shook hands civilly as the rest of the men poured out of the house.

Carter responded, "You know, Chief, I was just

thinking about you the other day. I was wondering if someday I wouldn't hear from you." He smiled, and Brady could see kindness in his eyes, that and the respect that Brady himself had for Carter.

"I always knew this day would come, Brady. We talk about business these days, at least I do. But there is nothing like a piece of unfinished business to suck you right back in. So here I am." He held his arms out to the side, hanging on to his briefcase.

"Well, Carter, I'm glad to have you. But I'm going to tell you, son, you need to get yourself some clothes you can get dirty. I'm not real excited about the way you showed up here. You're going to get greasy and oily. Your hands are going to stick together with all that crappy glue stuff you use all the time, and I just don't want to be responsible for that cleaning bill, probably going to eat up a major portion of your share."

They both laughed, and then Brady did an unchar- acteristic thing, but the only thing that he could do. He grabbed Carter by the shoulders and gave him a hug.

"You look real good, man. Now I can sleep tonight, knowing that we got all the best people, all the people that we need to get this shit done." Brady sighed.

Carter nodded his head, "Amen to that, sir. We've got a hell of a squad."

The rest of the team greeted the newcomer. Enemario was especially impressed with Carter's Mercedes. "I got just the body shop that can stretch this thing out. You could make a work truck out of it, and just think of all the stuff you could add. You could make a little office in the side, put a bed in there. You could turn this Mercedes into a camper." Enemario grinned from ear to ear.

Carter studied the green metal flake beast in front of him. "You call that a camper, Enemario?" he asked.

"Nah. I call that the beast. That thing's for special effect. I don't want to take it camping, scratch up the sides."

"Then why the hell are you suggesting I do that with my car?" Carter handed the briefcase to Brady and pulled out a second nylon duty bag. "You better not touch my car, Enemario. Otherwise, you aren't going to get my little present I brought for you."

Enemario's hands twisted and writhed, fingers entangling themselves. He was so excited to look inside the bag. "What is it?"

"I got you the sweetest little drone, and you honest-to-God cannot hear it when it flies. I mean, you can't hear a thing. It's like a bird flying through the sky. And I got hooked up with this neat IR stuff. It can designate fire targets with a heat sensor that recognizes patterns. I got this kid, this genius high school kid back in Mississippi, who came up with this idea, this prototype, and I built him a shop. He can start cranking these out as soon as we need them. So I thought I'd bring one, make a present of it, and let you and the team play around with it. Then, if it's worthy, I might let you guys invest in it. Since you'll have a little discretionary cash."

Brady could see the team was beginning to gel already. Every single man was different, with a whole and completely unique set of skills. Though some skills overlapped, that's how they always did their best ops. He figured every single man they'd selected was probably close to genius. Brady knew he'd test at the bottom, but that didn't matter. He was technically in charge.

But these guys were going to make it work.

For the first time since the tragedies of years ago, Brady felt joy.

CHAPTER 7

RILEY HAD COMPLETED his research while Enemario and Brady spread out some of the gear and equipment they were going to take. The explosives expert printed out copies of deeds, transfers, corporate documents, and the list of sponsors and donors for the nonprofit that Esquivel Rojas had set up. Dragon Limited was high profile in the Fresno area, putting on several charity events for schools and several Catholic parishes. They purchased computer equipment and uniforms for some of the children in the parochial district, most of them Hispanic. Rojas, it was rumored, was going to be made Man of the Year in Fresno County.

Riley could not believe what he'd uncovered.

Carter's little drone was no larger than the size of a seagull and kind of looked like one. Less than two feet long, the delicate wings unfolded rather than the normal slotted drone design they were used to. The camera was in a tiny bundle on the underside of the bird, and just like he had described, the motor was silent when flipped on. It had a range of one hundred miles and a battery life of nearly four hours. But what was most unique about it was that it could convert from aerial daytime pictures to nighttime infrared images, and it could evaluate and target human subjects, rather than animals or moving mechanical parts.

Although it couldn't determine whether the human was a good guy or a bad guy, it had the ability to target only two-footed mammals, never pets, dogs, birds, or robots, which was a problem earlier versions of his drone had run into.

Carter was bursting proud at how excited Enemario got. He insisted the drone was a donation to the mission, but he teased the team that his research and development company would be a sound investment to put their earnings into.

Brady checked to make sure every man had a sidearm, Sig Sauer being the desired weapon of choice, and steps were taken to make sure their guns and ammo were well hidden. It was a violation to concealed carry in California. Even though they had supposed immunity, Brady still didn't want to get entangled in the local jurisdictions.

His house looked like an armament store, everything laid out on couches and tables. They had vests, a pair of coms for every team member plus a backup pair, night vision goggles, and special heat-sensitive gloves designed so they could pick up and throw a burning coal. Riley had already fashioned some "taffy," as he called them. The little explosive devices wrapped in wax paper looked more like Halloween candy than flash bombs.

Brady also went over the medic kit with John and sought his advice on anything additional to pack.

John had one piece of advice for him. "You know what I found working in some of these places? When kids are involved, it's a good idea to have candy suckers. Something to hand out to the kids. If we take chocolate, it'll be a mess of pudding by the time we get there. I say we stop by a dime store and just pick up a string of multi-flavored suckers to create some cheap good will."

"Roger that, John. Will do. I'll let you choose the flavors." Brady grinned and then gave him a gentle punch to the upper arm.

"You think I should bring some diabetic supplies?" John asked.

"I got Metformin in my kit, but I'm not going to bring insulin, if that's what you're asking. However, we should bring some test strips just in case. God knows what some of those girls have been eating. We could encounter all sorts of diseases. But I'm thinking

Penicillin and Metformin, those should do it. Doses of vitamin C, if we need to. I think we're good," Brady added.

Riley had covered the dining room table with paperwork. He explained the corporate setup that had been created, he had pictures of several wealthy donors, and he told the group he suspected most of these people were simply duped into making donations but were not part of Esquivel's operation.

"I did discover there's going to be a charity ball on Saturday. It's a regular black-tie event at the country club. I say we designate Carter here as our billionaire bachelor looking for love."

Everybody turned, looking at Carter, who grinned. "That's probably not too far from the truth, but what's the point?" he asked.

"Carter, we think you'd be the right person to sort of get chummy with Rojas. Let them know you've got some money to spend. Maybe we can create a story for you? You've got a couple of kids and your wife took off. You need help with the housework, and you'd like to pick up a pretty young girl, perhaps adopt her if that's what he's willing to do, and explain that you'd be willing to pay handsomely for her. It just might snag him," Riley said.

"I shudder to think that could actually happen," answered Brady with a jerk to his spine.

"I think it turns all of our stomachs," said Carter. "But if you think it'll work, I'm game. So that means I take my car, right? I sure as hell don't want to show up in the camper van you guys found or Enemario's green monster. That just wouldn't go."

Everyone on the team agreed.

"You get to wear a tux. Maybe we could convince you to make a little donation to his charity, get his attention?" Brady asked.

"Okay. It's all settled."

Tate entered the room and sat next to Brady. It was his way of telling his master that he needed to go outside, so Brady let the dog out. Tate went hard charging into the bushes, barking. Brady stayed outside to watch him, leaning against one of the railings on the front porch. The stars were bright in the sky, crickets were chirping, and he knew he didn't want to lose this place or not be able to come back to it. He allowed himself the luxury of imagining growing old, he and Tate together. With the money they hoped to raise, he'd stop his grows, just live off the land, and relax into old age. That is, if the world would leave him alone.

But one problem concerned Brady this evening. He was going to have to leave Tate behind. It wouldn't be fair to the dog to send him on their trip to Fresno, and it would be dangerous. But Tate was not the easiest to control. He obeyed Brady, but he wasn't sure the dog would mind anyone else.

The door behind him opened, and Riley stepped out onto the porch next to him.

"How are you doing, Chief?"

"I was just thinking about Tate. You sure Cassie, the kids will be okay with him?"

"I think they'll do just fine with him. You don't expect we'll be gone longer than a week, though, do you?"

"Well, if it's longer than a week, we'll have to come back. We just get the guy, we plan for the handoff, and we're done. I'm hoping it's that simple," said Brady.

"I'll give Cassie a call and make sure she's still okay with it. But I'm sure she will be. The kids would be thrilled."

"Remind her he might go after your cats. And then there's the rooster. I'm just warning you."

"Cassie will take care of it, and the only thing I worry about is the kids seeing it. But we won't kill your dog just because he kills my fucking rooster. Come on, Brady, you know me better than that."

Brady chuckled. "You're right there. I guess I have a hard time saying goodbye."

As if on cue, Tate appeared at the bottom of the stairs coming to seated position in full attention. He looked up at his master almost as if he understood he was being left behind.

"Come here, Tate," Brady instructed. The dog

obeyed. Brady sat on a chair and held his snout with both his hands. "We're going to be leaving you with some good friends of mine, Tate, and I want you to behave yourself, okay?"

Tate angled his head to the side, as if trying to listen, to comprehend.

"Damn but that dog is smart. I just get the feeling he knows what you're saying," whispered Riley. "You know, Brady, it wouldn't be a bad idea to settle down. I think Tate would like it. It isn't natural to just be alone your whole life."

"I'm not alone. I have Tate. And that's the only kind of tethering I want. I don't understand women, I'm not interested in their drama, and to be honest with you, I hate kids."

"Well, you're one mixed up warrior, Brady. But I respect your wishes. You got to want to be tethered, and that's when it'll happen. I just decided the love of a good woman was something I could handle, was something that would be good for me, not a complication. So why... Well, when I met Cassie, everything fit into place. It was the easiest, most beautiful thing I've ever done. And I'd be lying if I told you it was fun all the time, but Brady, if I could wish anything for you, I'd wish that."

"No, I only want my best friend, Tate, here. This whole valley, this whole hillside could go up in smoke.

I could lose my house, my grow, my vegetable garden, all my equipment, my cars, my trucks, everything, but I don't want to lose Tate. That would hurt. And that's about the most I can do, Riley."

"Well, I'm going to pray for you, Brady. I'm going to hope you have a future where you have a partner in life. Because it's natural, and you'd be a good husband. And a terrific father."

Brady looked at the stars, shook his head, and said, "Riley, you're a fucking liar. But go ahead and dream, if it'll make you feel better. Don't dream on my account, though. I'm all taken care of. If I can settle the score with Rojas, I'm going to be a very contented man. And jumping into the fray with all of you guys, well, that's just a Boy Scout thing. That's like extra gravy. That's like whipped cream and cherry on top of the double scoop ice cream cone, you know?"

CHAPTER 8

O N THEIR WAY out of town, they dropped Tate off in Lake County, which was one of the hardest things Brady had ever done. The dog sat in the middle of Riley's driveway, stoically waiting for Brady to change his mind and ask him to come join them. But that didn't happen, and Brady turned his back, mounted the passenger seat in Enemario's monster truck, and tried not to look in the side mirror as they pulled away. At the last minute, he chanced a quick glance, and the dog was still there.

"He's going to be fine," said Enemario. "It'll be good for him. Riley's lady will just spoil that pup. She's a smart little fox, and she'll keep him out of trouble."

Brady knew Tate could find trouble all on his own, and he was known for being willful but smart. "Well, there's no chance he can come with us, so I really didn't have a choice. But I told him I'd be back. And I got to believe he understood that."

"And you will."

Enemario's words hit Brady cold, and his guts nearly dropped down to his toes. All of a sudden, his resolve was waning, as if a shadow had crossed over his grave. He shrugged it off as pre-op jitters—only brought on because it had been several years since he'd been on one.

It was a long, boring trip back to the Central Valley, and Brady was already tiring of the scenery. They passed several miles of once-green and lush fruit-producing orchards that were now paper-dry with leaves brown and curled. The whole area looked blighted. Rows of once prosperous orchards now went fallow. The lack of water in the Central Valley put many farmers in bankruptcy. And then there were others, mostly foreign investors, who came in, scooped up the land at a good price, made their private deals with the water district, got the water they needed, and replanted.

It was the same age-old story, the cycle of famine and failure, boom and bust, farmers everywhere had to contend with. Added to the mix was the political fallout from forces in the cities—namely Los Angeles and large population centers in Southern California—and the needs of rural California, the Central Valley. Somehow, in this mixed-up world, more priority was given to the populations of sun worshipers in Southern

California than was given to farmers in the bread basket of the West. Hell, it was the bread basket of California and the west too.

But that wasn't Brady's problem. On top of everything else the communities in the Central Valley had to deal with, they had a monster living in their village. And that monster was going to be removed—by force, if he had to.

"We take them one step at a time, don't we, Enemario?" mumbled Brady.

"Roger that, Chief."

John drove the old camper Brady had purchased, which was the lead vehicle, since it had to amble at a pace not to exceed 55 miles an hour. The dang thing smoked too. That left Carter riding alone in his Mercedes, since Riley chose to ride with John.

They arrived in Fresno late. The group had stopped along the way at a famous steakhouse, savoring the luscious beef dinners and oversized portions of potatoes and corn bread. By the time they reached Fresno, everybody was trying desperately to stay awake. They checked into an inexpensive motel with three rooms side by side. Brady bunked with Riley. John offered to share a room with Carter, but Carter turned him down.

"I'm going to go stay at the Marriott down the street. Since I'm supposed to be a billionaire, I think that's where I would stay. You room with Enemario.

And thanks for asking, but I'll be just fine." Carter winked, got the okay from Brady, then took off in search of nicer digs.

The remaining four members of the team crashed for the night, agreeing to meet downstairs for breakfast in the morning.

Over pancakes, Brady gave Carter the phone number to the charity so that he could be entered in the auction. The fundraising dinner was this evening, so Brady instructed Carter to get himself hooked up, wander around the ballroom, and pretend to be interested in bidding on several of the auction items. He even suggested he donate his time to help with the setup.

"I just want you noticed, okay?"

"I got it," Carter answered as he stuffed a fresh biscuit in his mouth.

"So, Brady, we're going over to the house or the ranch?" asked Riley.

"We'll check out what's going on at the house first, just verify that Rojas is there. Maybe we'll talk to our little waitress again?" Brady answered. "Then we'll head over to the warehouse and see if there's any new activity going on. I want to see if we can maybe get in tonight and look at what's in those containers while Rojas is distracted with the events of this evening."

They said their goodbyes to Carter, who asked

Brady quietly on the side if making a donation would somehow implicate him in the foundation or turn into something he'd regret.

"Carter, you could give him whatever you can afford to, a few thousand dollars maybe? Sort of buy your way in, so to speak? But it is up to you. I'm not requiring that you do so, but it would help with your cover. Just do what you can to get noticed and gain entry. I'll try to get you reimbursement for the funds you advance. You want one of us as backup?"

Carter shook his head. "No, I got this. You guys go check out his house and the ranch. I know how to do this. I doubt I'll get myself into anything that I can't get out of."

Because the green monster truck was so visible, Riley, John, Brady, and Enemario all rode in the camper van. They patrolled up and down the prune yard district, Riley and Brady pointing out the guard tower located in the palm tree, the wiring, the cameras, and the armed guards who wandered in and out of the garden area by the blue fountain. The back entrance of the estate was wide open, and delivery trucks transported catering supplies, wine, and flowers to the house in a steady stream over that hour-long surveillance they did. When the gate closed, everyone exited the van. Brady pointed out the locations once more of the cameras and reminded everyone to avoid detection.

They split up into two groups, and Enemario went with John to see if he could gain entry to the rear. Riley and Brady returned to the van and monitored their comms.

As the two members were allowed inside the courtyard, Brady heard Enemario speaking Spanish to someone inside the kitchen. The woman was apparently a cook, because he heard references to produce that had somehow not been delivered. Brady's Spanish was so limited he wasn't quite sure what he was hearing, but it appeared to be a story about them not wanting to lose business of the master at the house. The cook or housekeeper was speaking very rapidly, giving the two men an earful.

The comms went quiet as Enemario and John returned to the van, and Enemario suggested they drive away.

"They are gathering things for the party tonight, and I guess there is to be a little reception at the house. They're going to be showing some of the foundation's children, who will be serving. It's all designed to solicit donations, as a fundraiser. But the orphans are going to be serving the party. I just can't believe this guy. He's exposing his awful crime to a whole room full of innocent people. I can't wait to get him off the streets," Enemario said with attitude.

"When does the party start at the house? Did she tell you?"

John stepped up to the plate. "I heard 10 o'clock, is that right?" he asked, looking at Enemario.

"Yes. 10 o'clock. It's the after-party. The dancing and the auction go on at the ballroom, but then this smaller group will come to the house. These are the select donors, and I'm hoping, Carter will ingratiate himself, to be invited."

"So we'll nab him tonight then," said Brady. "We'll get that son of a bitch. I'll see if I can get hold of our liaison and wrap this op up tonight."

"Amen to that," Riley added.

While Brady called Carter to give him an update on the after-party, John drove over to the warehouse.

A large semi-truck hauling a double trailer pulled in through the gates just ahead of them. The team continued past the entryway, parking near the entrance to an abandoned big box store. The afternoon sun was beginning to heat up, and in the next hour or two, the temperature closed in on 100, so they stayed in the shadows underneath the shade of trees. The group found an unguarded entrance on one of the chain-link sections. There had been a padlock and chain at one time, but all that remained was the chain. The padlock was missing. They quickly entered the compound while several workers began unloading one of the trailers. They had boxes of supplies, appearing to be a combination of produce, lumber, and appliances in large cartons. The trailer was disconnected, and the semi brought the other trailer next to it. Workers began offloading its supplies, loading them on forklifts and taking them inside the warehouse.

Brady told the group he was going to try to gain entry and take a look at the camper van and other vehicles also stored inside the metal building. They were to meet back at this exit in thirty minutes.

Brady followed the eaves of the warehouse, which was in shade, making sure there were no surveillance cameras tracking him. At one point, a forklift operator came close to his location but did not discover him.

Brady slipped inside the building through a door after he picked the lock and waited until his eyes adjusted to the darkness. Sunlight poured through the end of the building where the boxes were being offloaded, but in the section where Brady stood, it was dark. He heard whispering and movement behind him.

He squatted down behind a pallet of two-by-fours and plastic PVC piping and listened. They appeared to be voices of young women.

Since the women spoke Spanish, Brady could not make out their conversation. He decided to go get Enemario to help translate. He tapped the comm on his ear. "Boombox?" he whispered.

"I got you."

"I need your services. Back west corner of the

warehouse. There is an open door. I am in the shadows close to the wall behind a stack of lumber. Somewhere on the other side, I hear voices, women's voices, but they're speaking Spanish."

"You got it, Chief."

Less than two minutes later, Enemario silently joined him. The two men listened, and as the chatter began again, Enemario nodded. "They have just arrived. I am not sure where they are from, but they have just arrived from Mexico, that is for sure. They are confused, and they are promised work. They are told they cannot call home yet, and several are angry because of it. They have family back home who will worry if they don't hear from them. But they're stuck, until they're placed with families. And it appears that these girls are to be serving the party at the house."

"Any idea how many?" Brady asked.

"I hear maybe eight or ten ladies. Perhaps more. One of them complained she thought she was pregnant. Another woman consoled her and told her she was lucky."

"Someone is coming to pick them up then?"

"Yes, they are waiting for work. But several of the girls want to call home. I don't think they realize they won't be allowed to."

"They're coming for work then. They're *volunteering* to come."

"In a way, yes, it appears as though they're coming of their own volition. This surprises me. Doesn't it surprise you, Brady?"

"It does indeed. I'm going to take some pictures of these boxes with their source codes and tracking labels. Why don't you try to strike up a conversation, if you can?" Brady instructed him.

While Brady photographed the boxes piled high with appliances and auto parts, Enemario focused his attention on the girls. In Spanish, he greeted them, pretending to be part of the crew. The tone of the conversation was pleasant. He told them not to worry, that they were going to see a very beautiful home, or something to that effect. Brady could hear the excitement in the girls' voices.

Brady worried something didn't quite add up. He was not expecting a voluntary exodus from Mexico, even though the stories told to convince the girls to come were probably untrue. He had visions of them drugged or handcuffed or mistreated. These girls were coerced by the promise of making money, big money.

When Enemario returned to his location and they exited the building, he got the rest of the story.

"Several in this group are sisters, and they all come from a small village in Michoacán Province. Their families have sent them to be forward guard, to be housekeepers and cooks and nannies for wealthy

Californians. They've been told they might live in Hollywood or Los Angeles or some grand estate somewhere. They're told they will be working for very wealthy couples, and they've been told they will be paid very well."

"I didn't expect this, Enemario. But if Rojas is involved, these women are in danger."

"I completely agree."

"I've got everything we need here. I think our best chance of getting Rojas is going to be at the house. We'll need to get you a vantage point so you can cover our operation, and that might take some doing. So let's get over to the house and get set up."

"Suits me fine. I've been mentally practicing my shots. I hope I don't have to, but if I do, I'll sure as hell be ready."

Confident the rest of their plan would succeed, they headed toward Esquivel Rojas's residence in the prune yard district and hopefully a surprise, successful capture. With any luck, Brady thought, they could be heading back to Healdsburg by tomorrow.

CHAPTER 9

BRADY AND THE three others picked up Enemario's truck and headed over to the estate. Carter had signaled he was in the ballroom, mixing with guests and introducing himself to the visitors and staff. He gave them photos of several of the young girls who were serving refreshments and showing people to tables along the ballroom perimeter.

Brady asked if Esquivel had been seen yet, and Carter denied it.

"I sure don't like that. Must be running late. You getting any strange vibes, Carter?" Brady asked.

"Not really, but then I'm not plugged in yet. People are nice. I don't see much of a presence, but I'm assuming Esquivel just comes with a very limited entourage. There's a lot of people here, and there's some fabulous auction items. I might bid on a couple."

"Knock yourself out," Brady said, shaking his head.

Speaking to John and Riley, Brady requested they

all drop by the diner and see if they could chat up the waitress again. She had been rather friendly before, and Brady thought it would be a good idea to double check some of his intel.

They picked a parking lot two blocks away so as not to cause too much attention. The old bus looked funny next to the green metal flake monster truck of Enemario's, and Brady was reconsidering the wisdom of bringing the thing at all. The van, or the gadget mobile, was necessary, since they would need to be living in it for a day or two if that's what it took to do proper surveillance.

They split up into two groups again, Enemario walking in with John slightly ahead of Brady and Riley. He scanned the area but didn't see the cowboy with the white hat. He did notice the waitress working a table in the far corner. Brady indicated to the rest of the group he'd like to sit as close to that table as possible so she would come over naturally. He and Riley sat down, and within seconds, the helpful woman was at their table with a pot of coffee.

"No, thank you, ma'am," Brady said, protecting his mug with his hand. "It's a little late in the day for coffee. But I'll have a piece of pie," he said.

"Make that two," added Riley.

"All right, boys, coming right up." She sauntered off to the revolving glass case on the countertop, removed two pieces of pie from the already-plated remnants in the carousel, and made it back to their table in all of two minutes.

"You didn't request peach, but that's all we got," she said. "And they're so good nobody seems to mind. Tomorrow, they're going to have berry, so come back then, and better make it by early afternoon, because we usually sell out."

She started to walk away when Brady caught her attention.

"Thank you, ma'am. Say, we talked to you a couple of days ago about Mr. Rojas and his Dragon Limited?"

She hesitated, her eyes squinted slightly. Then she furtively searched the room, obviously looking for someone who might be a witness to their conversation. At last, she relaxed, dropped her shoulders, inhaled, and leaned toward them. Brady was all ears.

"I understand Mr. Rojas is leaving for Mexico tonight."

Brady was beginning to have that icky feeling that occurred just before an op was about to go sideways. He worked to keep his patience, keeping his voice soft, low, and conversational.

"That surprises me, ma'am. He's got this big party going on tonight. I got friends who were looking forward to shaking his hand, making his acquaintance."

"I don't know Mr. Rojas, but there are two girls who help clean the restaurant for the owner, and they sometimes travel with him when he's shorthanded. Otherwise, I wouldn't know. They've put in for a few days off." She shrugged and quickly glanced around the room again.

Brady used the opportunity to delve further.

"Are you concerned about something? Is something bothering you?" he asked gently. He didn't want to spook the woman with too many questions, and he figured he approached his limit.

"He is a very powerful man, and I respect that. I also don't want any trouble. You are not a friend, I guess, so you may not know Mr. Rojas is a very private man. I haven't seen you here until this week, so would you mind telling me why you're asking? Are you investigating him? Because he helps a lot of people here in the Fresno area."

Brady's senses went into high alert. "No, ma'am. I'm sorry if we peppered you with questions. I just drove a tremendous distance to help my friend attend his event, that's all. And if it's all for nothing, well, I had other things I could have done. But we aren't investigating him. We don't do that. I'm mainly a driver." Brady hoped that she bought the lie.

"Well then, let me tell you something. You won't find many people in this town who will speak ill of the man. He has a lot of powerful friends here. He is a very important for the economy. He works with schools and children, and he supports an orphanage in Mexico. He does all this gratis. Unfortunately, with the way the border is these days, there are many children who have no parents or have parents who have left the area in search of jobs elsewhere. He takes care of them and finds them homes."

"I can see why you and others would be appreciative of all he's done," Brady answered carefully. He continued to bore into her eyes for an answer. She was difficult to soften up and kept her spine straight, her expression completely neutral.

"Sometimes, he finds babies that are abandoned. There are lots of peoples here who very much appreciate his hard work. For me, I just try not to get too close to such important people. I—"

Just then, two well-dressed Latino men walked into the restaurant and sat at a table on the opposite wall. One of the men nodded to the waitress, motioning for her to come over. She was visibly shaken yet tried hard not to show it.

"Excuse me. I've got other customers to see to. I've told you everything I know." She sashayed over to where the two newcomers were and demonstrated a broad smile.

Brady and Riley shared a shocked expression between the two of them. It was Riley who spoke up first.

"I'm getting a bad feeling, Brady."

"I'm right with you, buddy. I don't like this at all. We better check in with Carter."

They took one or two more bites of their pie. Brady could tell Riley was having difficulty separating himself from the rest of it. He left a twenty dollar bill on the table, got up, and left without addressing the waitress, heading toward the van. Riley was right on his heels. A few seconds later, John and Enemario followed them down the sidewalk.

Brady walked around the edge of the van until it obscured any view from the restaurant. The four of them huddled.

"I got bad news, gents. Waitress says that Esquivel is leaving for Mexico tonight. He's going to make a very quick appearance at his party, and I'm not sure where is going to be the best place to catch him. I'm going to recommend, Riley, that you go over to the ballroom with Enemario and John. I will head back to the house. Whoever catches the first sighting of him, I just want to hear about it, okay?"

John objected at first, but finally, the team agreed and split up accordingly. Over the course of the next three hours, Esquivel Rojas never showed his face.

The event at the ballroom concluded, an announcer called out the winners of the silent auction items, and someone from Dragon Limited got up and thanked everyone for their time. A small group left to continue the party at Mr. Rojas' residence. John and Brady had been waiting just inside the compound walls, nearly ready to pull the plug on the whole evening when the group began arriving. Brady wondered what had held up the rest of the team. His comm squawked to life.

"About time, guys. So all three of you are coming over then?" asked Brady over the comm.

"Yeah, we're leaving now. We're just going to come in separate vehicles. Carter's got someone he's been talking to who's going to ride with him," said Riley.

"Feel free, Riley, to do the same."

"Nah. Carter has all the moves. I've been out of the game a little too long. I'm just the bodyguard."

Carter and a young attractive woman arrived first at the house with a crowd of other partygoers. About ten minutes later, Enemario's truck arrived, and though he knew the man was trying to be discrete, the motor's decibel level was off the charts. The whole conclave watched him park his beast a block away. Brady instructed Enemario to take up a perch in a scaffolding adjacent a new construction site, where stucco was being applied.

There was still no indication that Esquivel was there. Then, after another half hour, Carter messaged

Brady.

"Boss, I got some bad news. They just announced that the party's over. I got a few pictures, but there are only about five or six girls here, and I haven't seen Rojas anywhere. It appears he's already gone. I hate to say it, but I'm feeling like he got tipped off."

"Fuck!" Brady's blood pressure spiked. "Okay, Carter, are you going to have to take your ride home?"

"No, I'm fine. I'll meet you guys wherever you want. What's next?" Carter asked.

Brady needed just a few minutes alone to think. "We'll talk in a few. Meet me at the Flamingo. We'll hole up there for the night and see where things stand in the morning."

"You got it. Riley's on his way over to me now. See you in a few minutes."

When the five of them assembled, Brady examined their faces one by one and noted they all had the same expression. The optimism of yesterday and earlier today was completely shattered by the lurking feeling that something had gone wrong, the plans had changed, and now it was going to be more difficult to find Esquivel Rojas. They knew the score. Their mission had just amped up to a whole new level. They were going to have to find Rojas in Mexico.

He knew that was the last thing they wanted to hear.

"Gents, this is what we're going to have to do. We know the general location of his ranch in Baja, just outside the town of San Benito, about ten miles from Cabo. It's in the hills, not in town proper, but other than that, we're kind of shooting from the hip and extremely blind."

He waited for this to sink in.

"Now for some good news. I checked my bank balance this morning, and I've got more money in there, so we're nearly halfway. She didn't say she was going to do that, but I think she knows we may need some extra expense monies. I have no idea why, but I'm glad they're playing ball with us."

"So you're saying someone from her organization, whomever they are, is monitoring us?" Riley said after he spat. "I don't understand why they don't nab him themselves if they have all that intel. Or are we bait, Brady? Are we the sacrificial lambs headed for the slaughterhouse?"

"I don't think you have anything like that to worry about, Riley." He didn't want them to see it, but Brady had wondered that same thing himself.

"Riley has a point," said Carter.

John had a sour expression on his face, and Enemario was checking out the patterns in the stars overhead.

Riley's impatience was growing. "Fuck, Brady. Did

your lady mention Stanley? Because this feels like it's got Lt. Stanley's hands all over it. They hooked you with the promise of revenge, and now they're going to take you out for good. Ever think about that?"

"No, Riley. I haven't thought about it that way at all," Brady retorted. It was a partial lie, and he was getting angry. "I hope you know me well enough to realize I would never put you in harm's way and that I'm a better judge of character than that."

"And you could be just flat wrong, too," Riley continued.

"No problem, man. If you want out, you got it. I told you all, if at any time you were uncomfortable with things, I'd make it so you could drop out. I meant that. I hope you know that."

He studied each man, one by one. "If you're not one hundred percent on board, you'll be a liability to the team, mainly to yourself. You'll start doubting things. We haven't really begun this op yet, and already a couple of you are complaining—"

"Fuck it, Brady. I'm not fuckin' complaining. Remember what I told you last week? You're asking an awful lot," barked Riley.

"I agree. It is a lot. But so is one million fucking dollars," Brady answered. "Even split five ways."

John spoke up. "There's that, and the fact that Brady can get some closure—we all could. We don't do it for ourselves. We're doing it for Maggie. In her memory."

Brady was grateful John had the cool head tonight. Normally, he could control his reactions. When one of his guys questioned his judgment, he'd let it slide off his back, even thank them for bringing it up. But standing here in this parking lot tonight, Brady didn't feel in charge of anything.

Now he was losing control of his guys.

Riley finally made eye contact with him. "You call the play, Bones."

Although Brady was relieved, he wasn't going to stop the discussion.

"I say it's all-or-nothing. We all go or none of us do. I'll split what we've got in the bank right now, a little over $400,000, and we can all go our own ways. But if you want to hang in there with me for the whole event, then we'll be going into Mexico. After tonight, whatever we decide, that's it. I want your feedback and suggestions—all of them. But no more questioning the decisions we're making. Let me emphasize that. We're all making the decision as one unit, one team. If one of you is out, we're all out."

Brady knew they were thinking about his words because no one would look at him.

"What's the lady going to do if we quit and take the money she's invested?" asked Enemario.

"That's not the right question. It doesn't matter what she thinks. She could ask for it back. But that shouldn't be the way you decide. You understand?"

Several heads bounced in agreement. Riley was stoic, and then he also began nodding his head.

Brady added one last point. "What makes us unstoppable is when we all contribute to the outcome. We decide together, we gear up and get ready, and we follow the plan. That's the best thing about this team. We come up with a strategy. Up until tonight, we were just getting started with the surveillance, just beginning to formulate a plan, and we hoped to get him quick and be done with it. But you know how it is. The plan goes to hell with the first engagement of the enemy, right? The enemy gets a vote, and in this case, we have to go with Plan B. Got it?"

They nodded, becoming more animated. He could see they were tired, too. A good night's rest would be a wise move. But Brady needed confirmation they were solid.

"I need to hear it, gents," he prodded.

Riley suddenly came to life, standing tall, as if he was going to salute, which he never would. "Hooyah, Master Chief Rogers. I'm in. I can't wait to ride in that dump truck down all those bumpy roads. I can't wait to rid this world of one bad motherfucker. If I quit now, I'd not be able to look myself in the eye, let alone speak to my kids. Time to go save the day."

Several others mumbled something similar. Brady made sure to examine their facial expressions, every one of them. He was delighted to find they were all men of steel, true warriors, and they might have concerns or worry, but there would be no more talk of quitting.

"All right then. That's a green light, as in go."

Brady launched into some logistics he needed them to consider and help figure out.

"I asked earlier if all of you guys had your passports with you so nobody should have a problem getting into the country. It's getting out of Mexico with Rojas in tow that will be the problem. We should rest for the night and then start first thing in the morning. From now on, we maintain our cover. We'll all ride in the van, and we will be fishing buddies on a pleasure fishing trip, okay?"

Everyone nodded.

Carter grinned and parroted Riley's comment. "Going bumpety bump in and around all those potholes all over Baja."

The laughter was soothing.

"Be thinking about staying away from the federales," Brady reminded them. "I don't want any legal entanglements. That means we hang together, we watch our backs, we don't involve too many locals, and we just stick to ourselves. When we get there, I'll try to find us some kind of accommodations, and of course, we'll have to charter a boat. We want to look like real fishermen."

"So we're going tomorrow then? Leaving from here?" asked Riley.

"That's the way it appears, Riley. Does anybody have any questions or an objection to that?"

"Brady, no offense but I don't want to leave my car here," added Carter. "I'm cool with going with y'all in the van. But how about I drive down near the base in Coronado and leave the car there. It'll be a hell of a lot safer than here. San Diego is a decent place to fly home from, so if you guys don't want to hang with me or ride in the van all the way back to Sonoma County or San Francisco, it would work out. I'd like to make sure my car remains in a location where I'll find it when I get back."

Several of the men chuckled. Brady was quick with an answer. "Carter, that's a great idea. I might hitch a ride with you, if you don't mind."

Riley and Enemario feigned a protest.

"Same for me. I'll park my Green Machine on the base at Coronado, too, right next to Carter's."

"Suit yourself. I understand that."

Riley addressed John. "No offense, John, but I think you're riding the buggy down by yourself. I'll hitch a ride with Enemario, if you don't mind."

"Hell, not a bit. I get to listen to all my old tapes. I'll sing show tunes I sure as hell won't be able to when you lot are with me. I say we split up and—"

"Nope. You're overruled. We go as a caravan," corrected Brady.

THE NEXT MORNING, Brady and Carter hadn't said much to each other the first hour of the trip. Brady decided to break the ice a bit and asked about it. "Everything okay, Carter?"

"I'm good. I get into a zone when I drive long distances. I'm just thinking about all the business stuff I'm doing, got a couple new deals I'm working on. I mainly like to think when I drive. But if you want to have a little chitchat, you just go right ahead, Brady." He gave him a wide grin, and Brady felt like an idiot for asking.

He shrugged, settled back in his seat, and wasn't going to force the issue any longer. It didn't take Carter long to break his reverie.

"Boss, there is one thing that I probably should go over with you."

"Okay, shoot."

"I wanted to explain a little bit about Stanley and sort of what went on, what the history was. I didn't really get a chance to talk to you after the operation with Maggie got shut down." Carter glanced over at

Brady. "I know this is a sore subject for you, but I got to tell you a couple things."

"Go ahead. Get it off your chest." Brady crossed his arms and prepared himself.

"Well, you'd gotten shot, right? Just before that, we were ready to go in, and the whole team heard Stanley's orders to stand down. Everyone was looking at you, and if you went in, they were going to follow you regardless of what that jerk ordered. You always were the team's leader, regardless of how he tried to tell everyone he was. The men didn't respect him like they did you. The jerk was stopping you from getting Maggie. I was right there next to you, remember?"

"How could I forget?"

"I don't think it had anything to do with Maggie. It had everything to do with Rojas, and I got the impression that Stanley was protecting him. And there's another part, too."

"Yeah, I kind of lost it there for a second. I was going to go in. If I hadn't gotten that round to the hip, I don't know what I would've done. I probably would've gotten all of us killed. They were going to shut it down either by giving us orders or standing in the way. There was no way in hell Stanley was going to let us go in there for the rescue. And there were about three dozen bad guys to our twelve, so the odds weren't in our favor. But goddamn, I sure did want to get her. And I think about putting a bullet in that man's head just about every night, truth be told. So there isn't anything surprising you can tell me about Stanley, except that he's a saint or a really good guy or something like that. You can't tell me anything about Stanley that I don't already know."

The emotions came flooding back from the op that had been so dangerously truncated. The moment Brady got shot, he halfway thought perhaps somebody from his own team delivered the round, but that was crazy. Besides, the angle didn't work. There wasn't anybody from their side anywhere close to the compound where Rojas was. Not unless Stanley himself or somebody else was in collusion with the bad guys. While Brady had considered that, he didn't think an officer in the Navy would stoop to something so low.

Carter let him stew on that for a few minutes and then began again.

"What I'm going to tell you next, Brady, has to stay between just the two of us. And you're going to see why in a minute. Do I have your word?"

"You do. Goddamn it, Carter, would you please get on with it?"

"Okay." He gathered his thoughts, took a deep breath. "Stanley is an asshole. His father bought his commission basically. They have friends, wealthy friends, high up in the military. He was coddled and pushed through the Academy and got his commission. About a year before all this shit started between us, same as with you and him, I was at a bar in Palm Springs. I have friends who own a condo there, and I used to go there on weekends, play some golf, and hang out at the spa. This bar is called the Blue Ox. Have you heard of it?"

Brady looked at Carter with a huge question on his mind. "That's a gay bar, Carter."

Carter slowly nodded his head.

"I go to those sometimes." He paused and then continued. "It's what I do for fun. How I meet people. Meet guys. I keep it to myself, and I don't date anybody in any branch of the military. But yeah, I've been gay my whole life, and I've done a pretty good job of covering it up. It was easier for me that way."

"Sure. I get it. Makes no difference to me," said Brady. "You're a hell of an asset for our team, Carter. And I'm delighted you did so well, but what does this have to do with Stanley?"

"I started the rumor that Stanley was jealous of the patent I sold, the money I was making. He knew he didn't have anything over me, because if he tossed me, it really wouldn't matter, except that it was just damn unfair. I've always believed in what I was doing. I'd wanted to be a Navy SEAL for the past dozen or so plus years. I didn't think the fact that I was gay would make any difference. We've always served in the military."

"I get you. I know that to be true."

"But the one thing I haven't told you is Stanley's gay as well. I saw him at that bar one night. And he saw me. Damn, he looked at me like he'd wanted to stab me in the heart. I was never going to use that information against him, and he could never use that information against me or it would screw up his military career."

"But Stanley's married, Carter. He's got two kids."

"Happens all the time, Brady. It's not uncommon to have two lives running side by side. That's not me. But some men live that way and want to be good husbands and fathers. But they're still gay."

"That's why he wanted to get you tossed. He needed you out of the way, because you were a liability to him."

Brady was beginning to understand.

"Exactly. There was no other way he could think of to eliminate that threat to his career, even though I would never interfere with his life. I don't know why it took me so long to tell you. I just thought you should know. It's one of the reasons I wanted to come on this trip, to sort of have a do-over. We should have gotten Maggie that day and killed that asshole who took her. I'm real sorry I didn't help you out more or protect you or get shot in your place, Brady."

"Oh, fuck you, Carter. That was never going to

happen. I wouldn't have let it happen. But it does explain a lot. And I thank you for that. You never have to worry about this discussion going any further. You can take the top off that jar anytime you want. I'm not going to."

CHAPTER 10

BRADY HAD SEVERAL minutes to think about his conversation with Carter on the way down to San Diego. He couldn't imagine the stress his young, creative former team buddy had been under, having to hold onto the secret he revealed today. Even worse, a commanding officer that none of the men respected had gunned for him simply because of that fact. It was unfair, and Brady already held resentment towards Lt. Stanley, but this put it over the top. He knew, since he was no longer an active part of the SEAL community, he had to do something to right the wrong that had been done to Carter.

It didn't matter that Carter was perhaps a billionaire, which is what the rumor was. That didn't count. The personal cost the man had to endure was not right. And it indicated a culture in his former community that needed improvement—needed the light of day shown upon it.

It wasn't just a moral case, although that was certainly enough for Brady to act. A commanding officer, no matter what his sexual preferences, who imposed his will or abused another fellow warrior could never be trusted in the heat of battle. An officer like that could lead a whole platoon to their graves. An officer like that might try to run away from the problem, demonstrating a lack of courage, while leaving others to die. The SEALs were supposed to be the elite of the elite. Brady understood nobody was perfect, but to willfully try to do damage to another's career to protect your own ass was wrong. And it deserved to be punished.

Brady trusted Carter even more than he did before. As Carter had mentioned, it was one thing to be a black man raised in Mississippi. Even after the civil rights movement, there were lots of issues surrounding race that were just not supposed to be part of the Navy. The SEAL community was supposed to be devoid of politics, religion, or racial biases. They had men from all over the world who came to the United States primarily to become an elite warrior and fight for this country. It was wrong for somebody raised with a silver spoon in his mouth to take that freedom and dirty it with his own little petty games. Or let his own lack of moral conviction harm another warrior.

So Carter demonstrated to Brady his complete

strength of character. Yes, Brady'd grown up in Mississippi too. But Carter was a gay black man growing up in Mississippi. Even if he used his maximum imagination, no way in the world could he ever understand everything Carter had been through.

He respected him. Carter never complained, and he could have. He just went on and did his job, taking the highway exit when he could.

Brady showered and laid out his clothes for tomorrow, just as he used to do when they were overseas. He'd always been harassed by the guys for even setting out his boots with the socks tucked in, his underwear on top of his pants. It was as if he was dressing for a funeral or dressing a skeleton or "bones," as he was known. He lay on his back and waited for the weight and heat of the day to bring him sleep. He was craving another hot, wet dream about Maggie. He knew that wasn't a very healthy sign, but if it got him through the day and the night, the very long nights, it was good enough for Brady.

He remembered meeting Maggie at the hospital one time when he had to go in for some minor re-stitching of a wound that had opened and gotten infected. Maggie was talking to the wife of another SEAL, consoling her about her husband's injuries, and asking the young woman to stay calm for the sake of the baby she was carrying. That's when he guessed

Maggie was perhaps a doctor. Later, he found out she was a skilled doctor, and her specialty was neonatal complications.

He was waiting for his name to be called, sitting roughly six feet away. He'd taken a long look at her when Maggie didn't notice, but his heart had started racing for some strange reason. It was a very new phenomenon for Brady. And he made himself stare at the wall or anything that walked by to the right, because Maggie and the SEAL wife were on the left.

He listened to her voice, calm and soothing, confident, and caring. She hugged the woman and gave her a card, writing her phone number on the back.

For an evil second, Brady felt like snatching that card out of the young wife's fingers.

What the hell are you doing, Brady? You having a moment here? Is this a chance encounter you've heard about your whole life but never experienced until just this moment?

It had been almost as if his overly inked and muscled fairy godfather was shouting orders in the back of his brain, laughing at him, poking fun, but making him fully aware of the physical changes going on in his body. He sucked in air and tried deep breathing. Then he closed his eyes and tried meditating into those deep breaths. He could hear Maggie's voice over the inhale and exhale of his body. Her voice, his breath, his eyes closed. He saw them naked, and it was the most beautiful, intimate act, scaring him to pieces.

He'd stood up so fast the wife jumped and said, "Oh!"

He paid no attention and stiffly limped down the hall to the right, his hard-on giving him fits. He approached the reception desk, making sure his appointment was still coming up.

"Mr. Rogers—excuse me—Master Chief Rogers, you are approximately thirty minutes early still. You're just going to have to be patient. We have other people we are seeing." The middle-aged nurse was firm but not unfriendly. Her eyes spoke to him and demonstrated the kind of patience she was requesting of him.

He figured she had some experience dealing with big guys with tats used to doing all sorts of other dangerous things, not languishing in a hospital waiting room. It wasn't one of the things he was trained for. It was something he had to endure. Inside, he laughed at the fact that he was probably more comfortable on a battlefield than in a hospital.

Because in a hospital, he didn't know what was going on. On a battlefield, he at least had a chance to figure things out and often made the right choices.

He heard a voice behind him. It made his hair at the back of his neck stand out and the lump in his throat constrict him even further. But aside from that and his racing heart, his pants reacted all too familiarly, as if he was a boy of sixteen experiencing it for one of the first times. But he turned anyway, knowing he was on uncharted ground.

"Would you like some water?" Maggie said to him. Her red hair covered her head and shoulders in ringlets, strong and wiry, with definite attitude. He wanted to run his fingers through those copper loops, and he imagined what she'd smell like if he exposed her neck to his mouth. He held her gaze for probably too long and then watched her smile as she held the little cup up to him.

Her hands were shaking. The water trembled in the center of the cup, little circles developing, just like the ringlets in her hair.

Looking down, he reached for the plastic cup, and their fingers briefly touched.

"Thank you. I guess you can tell I'm not exactly comfortable in a hospital setting." He tried to make himself sound official. A senior enlisted man would be gentlemanly, proper, and in full command. But the command he was thinking about had nothing to do with the military or military protocol.

Her eyes twinkled as she angled her head almost in a frivolous manner. Her eyelashes fluttered. And he saw the white flesh of her upper chest breakout in red blotches.

She was nervous too!

"Well, this is what I do, and so I guess I do feel more comfortable here, but I could remember as a child being very scared. I know how intimidating it can be."

So you think I'm a child, huh?

"Well, thanks for the water." Again, he was masking by trying to act gruff. He tossed back the entire plastic cup of water in just a couple of gulps, squeezed it, and tossed it into the garbage can. "Just what the doctor ordered."

It was very difficult for Brady to walk away at that moment, but he had to, as some sort of self-preservation mechanism, protecting him from an unknown enemy. But she was far from an enemy, he thought as he languished in and felt consumed by the look and feel and smell of her.

Months later, the familiarity and command he would take with her body parched his mouth and got him hard even tonight as he was off preparing for another dangerous mission. It had been such a miraculous year they spent together in San Diego. Everything about her had been magic, and he couldn't get enough.

Today, he was coming back to the town where it all started. But he had no desire to go back to Scripps Hospital and relive it completely. It wasn't the hospital he craved but Maggie's pulsing, shattering body as he pleasured her to oblivion.

Again, his mind took him back to that first meeting. When he'd looked up at the desk, she was gone.

"Are you waiting for someone?" the little blonde, pregnant wife asked. He'd forgotten that he sat close to her. His head was in a completely different space.

"I'm sorry, ma'am. My manners."

"An apology is not necessary. I was just making idle conversation."

"I have a confession to make," he began. "I was listening to you speak to the attendant, the lady doctor. And—"

"Oh, Maggie? She's my neighbor and a good friend, but she's not a doctor. She's a neonatal nurse. Works upstairs in the nursery ICU. She's a good person. Going to be doing some volunteer work in Africa next summer. Places I'd never ever want to go. But you know—"

Brady saw the young woman was nervous and interrupted her. "What I meant to say was I heard you talk to her about your husband. He's a team guy, is that right?"

She didn't quite know how to respond. She began mumbling, and then Brady interrupted her again.

"I'm a team guy, too. SEAL Team 5. I'm Brady Rogers, ma'am." He held out his hand, and her very small hand barely squeezed him back in a limp and timid shake.

"My husband is with SEAL Team 3. His name is Jared Cooper. I don't know what else to say except that he got injured. It's his eye and perhaps affecting his hearing, so we're a little nervous that—"

She hesitated.

"Go on," Brady encouraged her.

"Well, Jared's here and not at the VA hospital because we don't necessarily want the Navy to know. So please don't say anything, okay?"

Brady smiled and understood completely the sentiment. He'd heard it a lot. It was his turn to reassure her. "The Navy really doesn't try to toss guys. If they're still active and useful, they'll work with them a while. If he loses his eyesight, that could be something else. But usually if it's from a temporary injury, he'll heal. They're very good here. You came to the right place. The Navy will eventually find out about it. There's no hiding it. But I wouldn't worry. We sometimes are short on heroes, and we're going through a spell like that right now."

She looked up at him with her sweet innocent eyes and thanked him.

Brady adjusted himself in his seat and stared back at the wall in front of him. All he could think about was the way it felt to look at Maggie, to examine the awesome colors of her fiery red hair, the willfulness and strength of her personality exuding from every single cell of her body, and the heat as his finger slide gently next to hers. He was hungry, thirsty, and packed with whatever was causing his heart to race. It was like he'd gotten infected with a contagious disease, and he knew exactly what the cure would be.

Brady just didn't want to grab that card away from the little woman next to him. He'd find a way. But he knew he wouldn't be able to think of anything else until he was able to be alone with her.

Later that month, he'd went back for a follow-up and ran into Maggie again.

This time, as she approached him, he dropped his guard, testing the waters a bit to see if it was a mirage or if she was happy to see him. All his bells and whistles were flashing, flaring, and vibrating. The closer she got, the more intense the screams inside his head projected.

"Well, hello there." That was as far as Brady was going to go until he knew she was as interested as he was. It wasn't difficult to smile at the woman who stood perhaps a little too close for comfort. She was unafraid. He could say even defiant.

And he loved it.

Bring it on, sweetheart. I can handle whatever you're going to dish out.

"Fancy meeting you here," she said softly, almost

sounding like she was out of breath.

"Yes. I'm here for a recheck." His own breathing turned ragged, just like hers.

"Oh, darn, and here I thought you came to see me." Her eyes danced, searching his face, examining his neck, the size of his shoulders, his biceps, even dropping down his sides to examine his fingers. Then she scanned him head-on, face to face. He saw in her complete acceptance. Maybe even a little bit of desire.

Could this be? Am I imagining this?

"Well, I was hoping to. Does that count?" He waited for her answer.

She rolled her eyes and gave him a coy smile, an alluring come-on type of smile, like he might get in a bar somewhere late at night over a drink. That kind of smile. But this was the middle of the morning on a sunny San Diego Tuesday. No alcohol involved. Just as intense.

"I would like you to buy me a coffee," she whispered.

"That would be my pleasure. I am going to be seen here in the next few minutes. Can you take a break after that?"

She looked down at the floor, her body wiggling, her head moving from side to side as she thought about what she was going to say. He was completely enchanted.

"*I* don't care if I'm supposed to take a break now or not. Would you break *your* appointment?"

"Is that an invitation?" He made sure to lower his voice, making it come straight from his chest.

"I think it must be." She blushed and then asked, "Would you tell me your name, please? I never kiss strange men."

Brady nearly gasped at her words. He took a very small step toward her, and then she closed the gap, her warm body leaning into his, setting his belly, groin, and thighs on fire. His hand naturally came up to her face, his thumb rubbed across her parted lips. He bent down and kissed her.

The hospital, the waiting room, the canned music, the intercom system, and those walking past all disappeared.

He learned in that single delicate moment that he'd do anything she asked him to do. He would follow her anywhere. He would take chances he'd never taken before. The world he'd known, which started out as a black-and-white film noir movie with all sorts of scary side effects, bloomed into full living color.

She fit in to that place in his heart he'd kept barricaded his whole life.

CHAPTER 11

S HE'D BEEN THERE with him last night, all night
long. Brady didn't think he slept more than a
couple of hours, and he really needed the rest. But
Maggie joined him in spirit, even though it was impossible. Somehow, he just was not willing to let her go.

Not yet.

As he stared at the cracks in the ceiling, the sun had
not yet broken the horizon, and he wondered, in the
dark, how long it would take before he'd be willing to
try being social. He knew that's what Maggie would
want. He told himself that was the logical thing to do.

But he couldn't. That was the symptom he was
afraid of the most.

Could there be another woman for him? The
thought gave him the chills. He knew the signs of his
unwillingness to let her go was dangerous, meant that
whatever disease was rolling around in his head was
getting worse, not better. In the confines of his little

green kingdom up in Northern California, that didn't matter. Tate didn't seem to mind, and no one ever came to visit. But now, things had shifted. He was going to exact his revenge on the man who had forever altered his life. Who had stolen his only chance at true happiness.

Until the mission was over, he wouldn't think about it anymore. He was going to focus on what was next. He'd worry about how long after that he wanted to live. If he decided to toss in the towel, and he'd had several friends who'd chosen that route, he'd have to find a good home for Tate. Maybe he could stay with Riley and the kids. Maybe the dog would be more flexible than Brady. Tate might be able to live on, unlike his master.

Brady sighed and threw his hands up under his head, just thinking, letting his mind wander. He was supposed to be controlling it. He was supposed to be the first one up, the one organizing and holding it all together. But he just didn't feel like it.

"Besides, who's going to care if I live a little longer?" he whispered into the ethos.

He rolled over on his side and stared right into her eyes. He loved her that way. He loved her because of all the dark days he'd had before he met her.

"Maggie," he said to the pillow, "I'm not going to stop today or tomorrow, maybe next week, but I want you to understand. I have to stop this. If I don't, I'm going to go insane, yet I can't stop thinking about you, talking to you, feeling you're right here. And you're not. Somehow, sweetheart, I don't think you want that for me, isn't that correct?"

As she did that very first day he met her, she frivolously moved her head from side to side, rocking her chest along with her neck. She inhaled one long breath then closed her eyes and let the glorious breath release from her lips.

She suddenly opened her eyes.

"You will meet somebody, Brady. And then you won't see me anymore. I will live inside of her. You will love again."

It broke his heart to see her tears, softly cascading down her cheeks. His hand extended to her face, his left thumb wicking away streams of teardrops. "Don't say that, Maggie, please. I can't ever love someone like you again. But I can work on it. It would be different, but it won't be like this. I will never have this again."

"And I'm telling you, Brady, you will," she insisted. "And that's when I'll be gone. It's a good thing, Brady. You don't have to prepare me for it. I will just cease to be. You will have your new life. And I know you're going to be happy. I will it so."

He always liked it when she did that. She had a way of dissing him, really cutting him off at the ankles, and him still begging for more. Anyone else who tried to do that would be a bloody casualty. But Maggie could slay him as hard or as softly as she wanted, and he would plead for more. If he was wrong, he begged for forgiveness. If he was right, he'd still beg for forgiveness.

"How did I get so lucky for that year, Maggie? What did I do to deserve it?"

Her hand appeared from under the covers, her palm pressed against his cheek. She didn't say anything. Just lay there, touching him, lovingly gazing into his eyes.

"I guess we're just lucky, Brady. Most people don't get to have this. You know what they say, better to have loved and lost than never loved in the first place?"

"I hate that quote. I absolutely hate it. I forbid you from saying it again."

She pouted and then very gently nodded her head in agreement.

A knock on his room door told him this morning's encounter with Maggie was going to end. He mouthed to her, "I have to go."

She pulled the sheets up to her chin then faded into the pillow and was gone.

"Coming." He pulled his pajama pants up over his hips, tied the draw string, and showed up at his door shirtless and barefoot. He didn't even check a mirror to see what was happening with his hair.

Peeking through the peephole, he saw it was Riley.

"Hey, Bones, you okay?" Riley asked.

"Just being lazy. No biggie." He stepped back, opened the door wider, and invited Riley inside. "I haven't tried the coffee yet. You want some?"

"Sure, although I usually can't drink it without cream."

"I'm the same way, sport, but I'm sorry. I haven't got anything."

While he waited for the coffee to percolate, he noticed Brady was showered, shaved, and ready to go. That gave him pause.

"What time is it anyway?"

"It's about 7:30. I tried to sleep longer, but I couldn't."

"Well, that's two of us then."

"You still dreaming about her?"

"None of your damn business." That made Riley smile.

"I called home about an hour ago and woke the whole household up." Brady knew that Riley had something on his mind.

"Okay, so what's going on?"

"God damn it, Bones, you can read people's minds, can't you?"

"Nope. I just looked at you all nervous and tossing about. You probably checked out the to-do list we created last night. It's part of your obsessive-compulsive nature. I have the same affliction most nights. Right?"

Riley nodded his head sheepishly. "When I first started thinking about doing this little vacation with you, I thought 'no big deal.' But I never expected all of us would be borrowing parts from the Navy and basically asking for trouble."

"That's the way it goes, Riley. I'm sorry. How's Tate doing?"

"Well, I'm afraid I have some bad news."

"Come on, Riley, out with it."

"I'm afraid Tate got the rooster." Riley delivered it straight, dead pan. He did not show an ounce of remorse, concern, or worry. It just was a thing that got done. Tate was an efficient killer of animals and never let them suffer for long periods of time. If smaller dogs and cats and other animals underestimated him, they would do so at their own peril. Brady could almost see the point of death.

"Don't tell me. The rooster—"

Riley helped him out. "It was a good death."

Brady chuckled. Then he burst out into a full-on laugh. It was so crazy, but the scene in his mind was diabolical.

"I needed that." Brady handed Riley his coffee. "Did you get *any* rest at all?"

"Shit, Brady, you'd think I was a schoolgirl. I'm nervous as hell. I never liked Mexico, even when I was in my twenties. And now as the years have gone by, well, it's just gotten more and more dangerous. With these cartels everywhere, they're just having their way with us. The odds are not in our favor."

Brady sipped his coffee and nodded. "I know what you mean, Riley. I wouldn't want to do this full-time. It's one and done. And then, you know, they could just forget about me, and I'll forget about them. I just need to close this tiny loop, this little unfinished piece of business, and then my life will be simple and complete."

"So, Bones, since we're doing all this character reveal, I must tell you, I was mighty ashamed of how I treated you yesterday. I had no cause to question your judgment."

"Riley, you had every right to. I think that's how we're going to make this work."

"Well, I just wanted to apologize. I wanted you to know, Brady, you're my best friend. I never expect to have that kind of a conversation with you again. It was wrong of me, and I was irritated for all kinds of reasons, but I shouldn't have taken it out on you. You're the one who's trying to hand me two hundred thousand dollars. I ought to be jumping for joy."

"Well, you got something to live for. That makes a

difference. You got something good, Riley. I'm happy for you, man. You're going to watch those kids grow up. The teachers and the other parents are going to think you're their grandpa when you take them to school. But that's okay. You got a good woman there, and I think she's perfect with you."

"Thanks, Brady. I do too."

"And I'm glad you're not pissed off with what Tate did."

"Oh, hell, Brady. That old rooster had it coming. Tate just took care of business, that's all."

Brady nodded and chuckled. "Yup, he does what we do. Or what we're going to do."

"So are you still communicating with Maggie's ghost? Does she talk back to you?"

Brady was okay talking about Maggie. He'd settled into the routine. "Almost every night," he answered. "Not ready yet to let her go. Someday, but not right now."

Riley was smart not to say anything.

"I should have stopped her from going that last time. She had turned down that position. But the gal who was supposed to go got pregnant. Maggie volunteered to take her place. And *then* she told me. I should have spent less time being angry and more time trying to talk her out of it. Then she wouldn't have been there."

"But did she ever do what you told her to do?"

Both men laughed.

"The most stubborn woman I ever met in my life. Who would have thought I would fall for a stubborn woman?"

"Nah, Brady. That's exactly what you're about," Riley whispered.

BRADY CHECKED HIS bank account one more time before they crossed the border into Mexico. The money was still there, and he tried to give the mysterious woman's phone number a return call. He just figured it was worth it to make contact, if he could.

But the phone was scrambled, probably routed halfway around the world. He didn't know where the woman lived or was calling from. And that was okay. Maybe she had a way of knowing he was trying to call her, but anyway, he was ready for the challenge.

They stowed their guns and electronics, all their explosive devices in secret a compartment built into the floor of the camper van. Secured by screws and then covered by laminate flooring, it would be impossible for anybody to discover what they had brought, unless they put the vehicle through an x-ray machine. Even a bomb-sniffing dog wouldn't be able to detect what they were bringing because the compartments were lined with lightweight aluminum.

Enemario and John had walked to a local market and stocked up on supplies, all the basic stuff, including a healthy portion of beer.

Brady asked them to get their passports out, while they discussed briefly what the story was going to be. Somebody in their group had gotten divorced, and they decided it would be Brady, and they would all celebrate together by going deep sea fishing in the Sea of Cortez. They were going to play it by ear. They didn't have any plans; nobody made any reservations so there wouldn't be any tickets or ways anyone could follow them other than just doing it the old-fashioned way—on the road. They would have their cell phones, but nothing to indicate that they're former or active military.

Brady cautioned them about dealing with the Federales, getting entangled with local officials, and not to show that any of them had much money to spend. In reality, they had several thousand dollars tucked into one of those compartments, just in case they had to buy information from a trusted source, or buy their freedom.

It took them longer to park the other vehicles and get permission to leave them on the lot at the Naval base than they anticipated. The Navy hadn't gotten any more efficient with red tape than they were when everybody was active.

Surprise, surprise.

The border crossing wound up being very anti-climactic. The U.S. side just waved them through, and the Mexican side took several quick looks, asked to board their van, walked to the back, noting the bedroom and the bathroom, and—without saying a word—passed them through as well.

The road reminded him of the stretch of highway that led to Fresno. The brown hills were dusty. There were only pockets of lush vegetation when a local resort seemed to just pop up out of the desert. Small foothills at the side of the highway were perfect places for bandits and bad guys to hide out or to stage a lookout without being noticed. It was desolate, lonely, and felt dangerous as hell. A huge feeling of foreboding filled Brady's stomach.

Brady knew this stretch of highway was very dangerous, so he asked John to push the speed limit slightly, but not enough to get stopped. It was a twenty-hour normal drive, so anything John could do to speed it up would help.

Occasionally, they would hold up American tourists coming south, but word had probably already gone out that these were guys on a trip, no women, and no physical possessions of any remark, so they weren't targets. That's exactly what they wanted to look like.

An hour after dusk, they entered the town of San

Benito, about sixty miles from Cabo proper. It also was near the ranch, supposedly, nestled in the foothills overlooking the town. They decided to walk the cobblestoned streets, looking for some clean place to have dinner, and see if they could pick up some intel on where this ranch was located.

The bars were well-populated with American tourists. Only a few family units were present. Most were single males or couples, but it didn't even closely resemble the tourist-rich areas of Cabo. It resembled Cabo's older, washed-up sister, her bloom long gone and struggling to remain relevant. Alcohol flowed freely and generously. They passed gamecock shows, all sorts of freak shows, strip joints, and oddities that made Brady's skin crawl.

Riley thought it would be a good idea to ask about where they could pick up girls. One of the bars had a back room where certain services were provided. There wasn't any romance involved, just beds lined up and ready for customers. Even the bedcovers looked dirty. After they were ushered into the small, dark room, the door closed behind them and locked with a loud click. It was beginning to feel like an involuntary encounter. Brady's radar punched full on.

They were asked to sit on stools while girls paraded in front of them one by one, turning to the right and the left, not smiling, most of them young but appearing to be of legal age. All of them were either drugged or so stoned they had long ago shed any sense of caring for their personal safety. Maybe that was the come-on, Brady thought. Maybe some men liked it that way.

He stuffed down the bile developing in his gut.

Riley whispered something to the gentleman who had ushered them into the room. The man nodded his head, and as the group of ladies were ushered out unceremoniously, another group came in. These girls were very young, some as young as ten or twelve years old, even allowed to dress like the children they were.

And they were not happy campers. Brady knew their little scared faces would haunt him for years.

Brady could feel anger rising, boiling in his veins. He knew his men were so offended they had a hard time playing the parts they were supposed to play and kept looking to him for guidance. He was all out of ideas. He just didn't want to be there any longer. It seemed like a personal violation not only for the girls, but for himself and his team as well, and they were only sitting there looking at these poor souls.

In the long run, all they could do was tell the host they were not interested in any of the girls, which would lead to them being led from the room. But it was hard for Brady knowing these girls had probably been trafficked, sold into sex slavery to benefit some crime figure, and that, tonight, he could do nothing.

As they were leaving, one of the young girls reached out to Brady and held his hand. She said something to him in Spanish, and Enemario rushed to his side to translate.

"She says, please, Mr. American, she needs to earn some money. She would do anything you ask. And she's very good."

Enemario listened further, looked down at his boots, and swore. "She says they will beat her if she does not work."

Brady looked at her little hand in his, and he placed his other hand on top. "Tell her I'm sorry, but I am not that kind of man. But I wish her good luck."

As Enemario translated, Brady noticed this girl had a tattoo of a dragon on the underside of her forearm. He interrupted the translation, pointing to the tattoo. "El Dragon?" he asked her.

"Sí, sí." She ran off a string of words in Spanish once again, and this time, Enemario spoke back to her.

"Boss, she says that if you do not like her, she has a younger sister at the ranch." Enemario's eyes got wide as he emphasized the word *ranch*.

Riley sucked in air behind them. "*Younger?*"

"Tell her we would like to visit the ranch. Ask her if El Dragon is there."

During the translation, several of the other girls surrounded Brady. All of them showed him their dragon tattoo as well. It seemed to be their admission ticket to whatever dangerous game they all were playing.

The door to their little room burst open, and their host yelled at the girls, who scattered and exited through another door on the other side of the room. He said something to Enemario, who nodded. Brady heard the word *rancho* and was heartened. But his teammate was greatly affected by the brief words he'd exchanged with the stranger. Enemario clammed up and wouldn't look back at him.

Freed at last, they wandered casually down the street. Cars and bicycles rattled as they passed by, bumping over the old cobblestone pavers. Enemario waited until they were well clear of the little bar before he turned and addressed the group.

"Gentlemen, we have a formal invitation to the ranch, tomorrow at nine. He said that we will find whatever it is we're looking for there, 'as close to paradise we will ever come.'"

Riley wanted to know if they needed directions, what road they were to drive tomorrow.

"No, we are to ride with them in their trucks."

Carter, who had been rather frosty this morning and neglected to engage in even simple smack talk, gave a small opinion.

"Brady, I don't like this scenario at all. It just

doesn't feel right. They didn't ask anything about who we were or what we did or why we were here. That's not normal. It's almost like they know who we are already. Like they were waiting for us to show up."

CHAPTER 12

I T WAS NEARING 9:00 AM. Brady tried to eat some breakfast, but Riley shoveled down more food than anybody thought possible. With a chip on his shoulder, Riley chastised them all. His mouth was full of corn flakes and milk.

"For all you know, we're going to be stuck in some hole for a while or carted off to jail. I'm going to get one good American meal in before they grab me. So, if you don't mind, bug off."

Brady shared a long glance with Riley, and his buddy shrugged. He set down his spoon and further explained.

"Look, Brady, I'm sorry. When I get nervous, I eat. I'm just not wired up for waiting."

John had been reading a book, sitting on the bed at the rear of the camper. "You think you're the only one nervous, Riley? Hell, we just all show it in different ways. I've got myself a little sci-fi. Carter over there?

He's looking at poetry. Love poems." John wiggled his eyebrows up and down to make a point.

Brady was sensitive to the information he had about Carter but didn't react, because Carter chuckled.

"Yeah well, John, I read beyond a third-grade level. While there might be some science fiction I like, your idea of science fiction is graphic novels. And I'm sorry, man, don't mean to diss you, but that's just not me. Growing up in Mississippi, we called them *comic books*. It's all you white folks out here who call it *graphic novels*. And that's BS."

He followed it up with a wide grin and a belly laugh, and soon, everyone was doing the same. Even John winked at him, nodding.

"Touché. You got me there, Carter."

Brady needed some air so stepped outside, surveyed the dusty gray hills, and wondered to himself why anyone would voluntarily live in this part of the world. He didn't even like Palm Springs, and that was beautiful compared to this landscape. Arizona had lots of color, beautiful rock formations, and mountains. Palm Springs had those beautiful trees, oases, and golf courses. This place reminded him of Bakersfield. And Bakersfield was famous for just being one huge truck stop.

He noticed a trail of dust coming their direction several miles away. They had parked for the night under a couple of large trees that had survived several drought years, half their foliage dead and half struggling to stay grayish green. There were lots of coyotes nearby, and they heard them howling all night long.

The road leading to San Benito was only about a quarter mile, but the local brush and small foothills, dotted with large boulders like the surface of the moon, obscured the town from view. As he continued surveying the area, the dust streak got larger and larger. Two black Suburbans came into view.

"Guys, our escorts have arrived."

The other four members bailed out of the van.

"Remember what we talked about, and this is a do-or-die situation. We aren't going to do it any other way, okay?" Brady reminded them.

"Gotcha," said Riley. Others nodded and mumbled their approval as well.

Without any consideration for their comfort, the two Suburbans pulled up in front of them, enveloping the five former military men in a cloud of brown dust. Several men got out of the first Suburban, leaving the second and third doors open, while the driver left the motor running. One man got out of the passenger seat of the second Suburban. They pointed to the doors, but Brady's team didn't move.

"Enemario, it's your show now."

Enemario asked if anybody spoke English, and surveying the unfriendly faces, Brady understood that either they didn't speak English or they were unwilling to say so. Enemario began his negotiation.

Right away, one of the men, a heavyset grey-haired ranch hand who was the best dressed of the bunch, began shaking his head and blurting out, "No, no, no. It's not going to happen that way," in accented English.

"Then I guess we're going to go down the road a bit and find another place," Brady answered them back, his hands on his hips. He continued, "Look, fellows, we're just here for a good time, and we've heard all kinds of stories about this area, and we don't know you from Adam."

"But you asked for El Dragón. So apparently you are acquainted with our practices, and it is always done this way, señor."

"Yes, we were told to ask for him, but we've never met the man. And all of us here are a little bit concerned and edgy about going in a vehicle in a strange place with men we don't know. So you're going to have to forgive me, but there is no way in hell we're going to get into your vehicles." Brady pointed to their camper van. "I don't see any reason why we can't drive our own vehicle. We have everything we need, and if my understanding is correct, it's not very far from here. Perhaps not all of us are going to be interested in what your ranch is offering. So this gives us the opportunity to remain comfortable in our own environment. If you don't like it, then you can tell Mr. Dragon, or whatever the hell his name is, that his hospitality sucks and that we're no longer interested."

Enemario gave Brady a stern scowl, whispering, "I am not sure this is wise. Maybe we should try to just go along with him. Maybe some of us go, and some of us stay in our camper?"

Enemario was playing the part they had all re-hearsed.

Brady feigned insistence. "No. I'm not going to do that. You guys are here to help show me a good time, right?"

Everybody nodded.

"This is my rodeo, and if I don't feel comfortable here, I'm not going."

The heavyset ranch hand who appeared to be in charge put up his finger and pointed to his cell phone. "Let me ask the boss. If he's okay with this, no prob-lem. Otherwise, we have rules, and it's for the safety of our employees, I'm sure you understand."

Brady agreed.

The gentleman walked slowly to the other side of the first Suburban, engaging in conversation lightly out of earshot. Enemario indicated with his hand that he couldn't pick out a thing. When the gentleman re-turned, he smiled, revealing a large gold canine tooth.

He really looked more like a jackal, Brady thought.

"It has all been arranged. Señor Dragón has agreed you may follow us in your vehicle." He gave a quick order to the men standing around him, who climbed back into the vehicles and waited, with motors running.

Brady and his team boarded the van, as John pulled out and followed behind.

"I didn't think you were going to get your way, Brady," said Riley.

"And I was prepared to walk away. That's what you do in the marketplace here, right?"

Enemario looked disgusted, with his arms crossed. "These are not normal people, Brady. They don't like this show of force. They don't respond well."

"You of anybody should understand we don't get to play victim here. We're here to do a job. And I'm not going to allow the team to take any unnecessary risks or get into a situation where we have no control. I'd rather pull out than go along with their demands. I'm sure there's going to come a time where we won't have control, but for right now, we're setting the ground rules. And remember, I don't want to be separated from our money or our firepower. And none of you should be, either."

Riley nodded. "I'm with you there, boss."

"Me too," said Carter.

John also agreed.

In less than five minutes time, the van turned off the dirt road and traveled on a perfectly paved driveway that snaked up a small foothill ahead of them. As they got closer to the top, an expansive and perfectly manicured villa appeared. It was fully fenced, but the fencing was shaded in large flowering bushes of oleander and hibiscus. There were also tall flowering locus trees, palm trees, and several other plumeria and bougainvillea bushes. The whole beauty of the estate was ten times more impressive than the one in Fresno.

Groundskeepers actively worked to trim lawn and trees and pick up debris. Armed guards walked past the gated openings of the courtyard, and the sprawling building complex had views of a valley beyond that was not visible from the roadway or the approach to San Benito. Below was a vineyard, a huge lake, and a lush open pasture dotted with horses.

John was directed to pull the vehicle next to the two Suburbans that had parked, and they were ushered through the guard gate into the courtyard beyond, walking under a bougainvillea-laced veranda filled with chirping birds, and into the back entrance of the house. None of Brady's men said anything at all, and Brady was frankly surprised at the level of organization and the stunning setting. Obviously, times had been good for Mr. Rojas.

Through a large cafeteria-style room off the kitchen, they passed by an older woman on her hands and knees, scrubbing the floor. She barely looked up before they were ushered down a wood paneled hallway littered with pictures of Mr. Rojas on various horses or standing in front of prize bulls with large blue and yellow ribbons held up in front of him. There was also a picture of a large fiesta taken at the front part of the property, appearing to be an employee type of event. Smiling faces were in abundance. Everybody they had passed along the way, except for the gruff men who came to pick them up, belied an idyllic working situation. Men and women were lucky to find their jobs and wanted to keep them.

The older gentleman opened a set of carved walnut doors and ushered them inside a private office with an enormous wall full of books. The ceilings were coffered, also paneled in carved walnut or mahogany. All five leather seats were lined in a row in front of the enormous desk that was easily fifteen feet wide. Behind the desk was a reclining chair covered in brown and white spotted cow hide.

But the chair was vacant.

They were left alone, so Brady used the opportunity to remind the men that they were probably being closely monitored.

"I believe I see four cameras. That means there's

probably at least another four where I can't locate them," he whispered low and slow.

John added, "I see one in the clock in front of you. I see another in the ear of that buffalo head hanging over the opposite wall there." Everybody turned and looked into the eyes of a genuine stuffed bison bull.

"Well, I certainly didn't expect this," said Riley. "I've never seen such a massive and beautiful setting. I can imagine he enjoys living here."

Enemario shrugged. "Where are the dragons? I expected to see those."

The team chuckled, nervousness taking over.

Brady thought about Riley's comment. "A man of considerable reputation and wealth must have a place where he can relax and kick back. This is a fortress. It also could feel like a prison to some."

The door behind a large wooden file cabinet opened, and an attractive Latina woman, about forty years old, walked in. Dressed in a navy-blue suit with a white collared shirt and long sleeves peeking out from under her cuffs, she looked professional. Her hair was up in a severe tight bun, and her eyes were framed by blue glasses. They all stood when she approached the desk.

"Gentlemen, please take your seats." She bowed quite formally, gesturing for them to seat themselves. They quickly complied. Then she sat.

"I am Evangeline Rojas, Esquivel Rojas' sister. I help him run the rancho when he is gone, and as he is attending his niece's wedding, I have been tasked to greet you and show you what we have here."

Enemario began to address her in Spanish, even though she had spoken to them in perfect English. She stopped him, exposing her outstretched palm.

"Please, only in English."

"Very well. Your brother has a great reputation. I have some cousins in San Diego who recommended this house is a special refuge for my friend here, who has gone through a recent divorce. I was told this place is where wealthy men could come and experience something they perhaps couldn't experience in California."

Evangeline raised her eyebrows slightly and nodded her head. But she waited for Enemario to continue.

"First, I need to clarify something. We are not wealthy clients or businessmen. We are working men. But this is a special occasion for Roger here, and we all are willing to chip in so he can have an experience. It has been a very long and arduous divorce."

Brady had to look at his shoes. Enemario had been doing such a good job acting his part that he was going a little bit too far, and Brady felt like he was going to explode in a peal of laughter. Watching Riley cross and uncross his legs several times, Brady picked up that he felt the same way. So he created a pattern interrupt.

"Ma'am, they tell you that it's for me, but it's really, you know, I think they want to have some fun too." Brady grinned at his buddies as if looking for confirmation.

Carter was not happy. Brady noticed that he felt very ill at ease. Part of this had been staged so he could monitor everything from the vehicle, record the rotation of the security for the ranch, and be available in case something horrible and unexpected were to occur. He'd be joined by John while Riley and Enemario would stay close to Brady, the guest of honor.

Evangeline Rojas seemed to also notice Carter's sour demeanor.

"And you, sir? What about you?"

Carter leaned back in his chair and drilled her with a look that even surprised Brady. "I'm going to be manning the van, ma'am. I'm going to wait there if you don't mind. This isn't really my thing. It's for my friend here."

Evangeline shrugged her shoulders and gave a brief acknowledgement with her forehead. "We operate something special here. All our girls are different ages, all different races, and from many different countries too. Many of these girls have come to us as orphans, street kids, some of them addicted to drugs. Some of them come to us sick and starving, having been abandoned or kicked out of their houses or left penniless. My brothers and my foundation, Dragon Limited, take these women and restore them to health. We teach them courage, just like a fire-breathing dragon. They are seen by doctors, well cared for, and we help them get on their feet. Some of them meet husbands and go off and have a wonderful life. In fact, we encourage it."

Brady's anger was rearing up, getting ready to explode.

"What I'm telling you is that these women have been completely rehabilitated. They take their legal and registered profession seriously, and of course, the more experienced women are a little bit older. We don't encourage young girls into this profession, of course, but we also run a school and an orphanage."

She paused for a few seconds, assessing their reaction.

"Occasionally, our women get pregnant. And if they want to keep the baby, we allow this. We pay for all their medical bills, and we make sure the baby is well cared for until she can care for them herself. My brother has won lots of awards for his humanitarian efforts."

Brady was stunned. It was certainly a new wrinkle on the oldest game in the world. They were definitely running a house of prostitution, but they were also running a baby farm.

He was glad Rojas was not sitting across the table. He was glad it was his sister instead, because unless attacked, Brady would never willingly attack a woman. Rojas, though? This night would be his last on earth.

CHAPTER 13

THIS PART OF the plan diverged when Rojas didn't arrive at the ranch. The idea was to make the appointment for Brady, just so they could get inside the compound without resorting to violence. Once inside, they'd grab their mark, drag him out, and then drive away. Of course, lots of things had to happen in the meantime, like covering the escaping parties, setting incendiary and explosive devices, and using their new drone to drop small flash bombs for enhancing the confusion. They hadn't anticipated that Rojas' sister would be the one giving them their tour.

But Carter and John retired to the van, just as originally planned. Enemario and Riley remained close, chatting with some of the help and turning down offers by several of the ladies who were there. Their job was to collect intelligence, especially Enemario, who could listen to private conversations in Spanish. If they could, they wanted to connect with someone on the staff who might be dissatisfied. Someone who would help them.

So far, Brady was told, that hadn't happened. But they were going forward anyway with what they could do. All they needed was one little break, a tiny miracle, and their fortunes would change. No one was giving them information on when Rojas was to return, either. It was a guess. This part of it was frustrating to the team.

With all that in play, Brady was led to another room and asked to wait. He knew this was going to be difficult, trying to convince someone who was an innocent, but very much involved in the business, to help him. He wasn't sure he'd get much cooperation. But the hardest thing for him to do was be cruel or mean or demand help from the woman he had chosen to see. He picked one who looked extremely young, perhaps slightly underage. A younger girl would be more susceptible to help him. The older ones might know the score a little better and report him.

The door to the bedroom opened slowly, and the pretty little thing who marched in didn't look anything like the photograph. In fact, Brady was certain she was a different girl altogether. She was probably no more than about fourteen years old, way under five feet tall, like a true child. He found it challenging to even look at her; he was so ashamed she thought of him as a pervert. But he pressed on with his mission, which was to convince her that he could help her escape, and he honestly believed he could.

She was barefoot, dressed in a white smock. Her long, silken hair shone, freshly brushed. She wore hot pink lipstick, which was so out of place on this young woman working in such a dangerous profession, if it could be called that. Brady hoped she had a gentle, innocent spirit and was perhaps going to be more trusting than most. That was a good sign.

When she approached him, she took his hand.

"Would you like to come to the bed, Mr. American?"

"Roger. You can call me Roger." They had decided as a team it would be easier if he used his last name.

"But we should go to the bed now. I have things I can show you."

Although she was trying to pull him up to standing position, he remained fixed in his chair. He pointed to a small settee about four feet away from him.

"I'd like you to sit down, please, and I'd like to talk to you for a few minutes first."

Her eyes grew big like saucers, and then she frowned.

"No, please, Señor. Did I do something to displease you? If so, I can get—"

"No, sweetheart. It's not that at all. Just hear me out a bit. We need to talk."

"I am responsible for earning my portion of my rent, and I have a sister. I don't have time to talk."

"But I'm paying you for some of your time. So I'm paying you to talk," Brady insisted. He checked that his voice was gentle and calm.

The young girl searched the room carefully, as if someone were standing there. "This is not a good idea, Mr. Roger." She pulled the settee toward him and whispered in his ear, "They are watching."

This didn't surprise him. Besides, this kind of recording could be a second source of revenue for Rojas. "I understand. Now please sit back down. I don't want to hurt you, and I don't want to get you in trouble. Do you understand?"

Brady tried to speak to her as if he were a relative or the father that probably never really cared about this young girl. It wasn't hard for him to imagine having a child like her. His moral indignation was giving him fits. If he could, he would have snatched her and set her free.

She sat down carefully, her knees together, her hands folded in her lap after pulling her hemline down to cover her legs properly. She looked positively angelic, which was probably the whole idea.

"I came here to find out about Mr. Rojas. If you help me, I will help you," he whispered.

"No, Señor. I am very happy here."

"So how long have you lived here?"

"I don't remember when I came. I was little. I don't remember my parents." She didn't act with any emotion. He was surprised to hear that living here at the ranch was all she'd ever known. "There are many of us children who live here, and we have a very nice life. We work in the garden, we pick fruit, we help with the horses and the animals, and we play together and have fun."

"But you're not allowed to leave the ranch, is that correct?"

"Some do!" Her demeanor brightened. "Some get married. And they leave to go meet their husbands."

"Meet their husbands? How do you meet your husbands?"

"Today, there is a big wedding in San Diego. Mr. Rojas is there."

"Yes. The wedding of his niece?"

"In a way, yes. It is a big wedding, because several girls are getting married today. They go to meet their husbands."

"So Mr. Rojas arranges for them to meet men, who then will marry them. Is that what you're saying?"

"Yes. Without Mr. Rojas, we wouldn't be able to meet anybody. He has been very good to us. I have an older sister, and she is one of the lucky ones who is getting married today."

"Does your sister have any say in this wedding?"

"Of course, but why would she object? Mr. Rojas finds us husbands who are very wealthy, with big houses and beautiful cars. These new brides go live very happy lives. I hope he will find a husband for me as well."

Brady sat back and stared at the ceiling, trying to think of all the information he needed. He didn't want to spook her with too many questions, but they'd come to Mexico to catch him, and now it appeared there had been a change of plans. He wondered if somehow Rojas was onto him.

"So Mr. Rojas will be here tomorrow? This was all planned ahead of time? And does it happen often?"

"What does that matter? My sister is delighted, just like all the other girls who came before her. She is free, living in a new country with a nice husband and money to spend on her own. I want that for myself as well."

"I'm sure you'll find that someday—what did you say your name was?"

"Isabel."

"Isabel. That's a pretty name. So these weddings, your sister has planned for this I imagine for a long time. Does she know this man she's marrying?"

Isabel frowned. Brady could see she was getting spooked, and he cursed himself inside for rushing thing. But time was ticking away. He maybe had one shot at this, and then his real intention might become discovered. He needed to be careful not to blow it.

"Just tell me what you can, please, Isabel. Perhaps I might want to do something like that. Could you explain how it's arranged?"

She examined her entwined fingers on her lap. With hesitation, she told him her sister had left only a week ago, after it was announced she would be getting married.

That's exactly what Brady suspected.

"She lived here with you."

"And with her daughter."

"She has a child?"

"Yes, she has a little girl, three years old now. I take care of her."

There was a lot to unpack here, but he needed to go further. "How did that happen?"

She smiled. "Surely—"

Brady interrupted her. "No, I didn't mean that. I meant how did she manage to get pregnant? Didn't she use protection? Or was this a planned pregnancy?"

He thought for a second perhaps he'd gone too far, but Isabel had a quick answer for him.

"She was a gift from God."

"Someone she knew then, someone she planned to be pregnant with."

"No, Mr. Rogers. It was a miracle. One of her customers gave her a little gift when she wasn't careful."

"I'll bet her employer was angry."

"No, he was very happy. He told her that he will make sure the baby had everything she couldn't do for her and would send her to her new home after she was married. El Dragon is a wonderful man, a gift from God."

Brady clenched his teeth but otherwise showed no reaction. Isabel was watching him carefully now.

"Well, I'll find out from Mr. Rojas how all this is done. And did you say he'd be back tomorrow?"

"No, I think no. Tomorrow is the wedding. Tonight is the fiesta." Her eyes lit up like tiny sparklers.

"And do you know where this big wedding is going to be?"

"It's always at the Cinderella Slipper. That's in San Diego. You know of it?"

Brady had frequented that motel in his younger years as a recently minted young tadpole. It was in a seedy part of town, an inexpensive place where lots of young, hopeful SEAL candidates could take a date and not blow a week's worth of wages. The area was known for street gang violence and robberies, so unless armed and with several other men, Brady hadn't gone there alone. And for the last ten years, never.

"So Mr. Rojas will be there another day, and then

he will come here?"

The young girl thought about his question, as something seemed to spook her. "Señor, I am okay talking, but I need to talk to you about me. Or about you. I will hear from my sister soon, I hope. She will call me in a few days, even if it's just to say hello to her daughter."

"Has this happened before—to other girls you have known here?"

"Yes, they call to speak to them. And when the time is right, Mr. Rojas will send her little girl to her. In the meantime, her daughter gets to stay with me, and I help my sister by taking care of her."

"One last question, Isabel."

"Oh, so many questions. I didn't expect this."

"But I'm paying for your time. Why wouldn't she take her daughter with her if she was getting married?"

"I think perhaps she wanted to let her husband get used to her first, and then he would soften and allow the baby to come. We hope that happens."

"Because he chose Isabel, but not Isabel with a daughter."

"I think so. She discussed this with Mr. Rojas' sister."

"I hope so too. For her sake, for the sake of the child." Brady studied her again, and as she looked up at him, she blushed. He could tell the big question mark in the air was why he wasn't interested in her, physically. He needed to have an answer for that. He began what he'd hoped would be the moment he could convince her to help him.

"I am looking for someone myself, and I was told that Mr. Rojas could help me."

"I know he can. There are lots of people who come here, who have a great deal of money."

As they spoke further, Brady began to understand that Mr. Rojas saw himself as a benevolent relative to all these girls. That's why Mr. Rojas' sister described the wedding as that of his "niece."

"Come. I must work or I will not get paid."

Brady had already shelled out close to a thousand dollars for this young girl, but he reached into his wallet and grabbed a few twenties.

"You take this. It's just for you. I want you to have it, and there's more, if you will help me. Wouldn't you like to go to the United States and meet someone yourself, fall in love with someone of your own choosing?"

"I'm not sure. This is the only life I've known. My sister told me she remembers being hungry all the time. I can remember what it felt like to sleep in a bed with many other children. I like living here, because I have a bed all to my own. I never have to worry about going hungry. I'm never alone, and my sister's daughter will be taken care of. And Mr. Rojas will protect me."

Although he'd gained some valuable information, Brady called a halt to the interview. He explained to her he had a medical condition that didn't allow him to "perform" and that he was exploring alternatives to a traditional relationship. He needed to discuss this with Rojas.

He knew now the ranch represented safety to this young girl, and the asshole who took Maggie away from him was like a favorite uncle or father figure in her life. There wasn't going to be much chance Brady could shake that loose from her, and all trying would do was expose his team.

"I would like to come back. May I?" he asked.

"Yes. But no more talking. No more questions, Señor."

Brady was led back through the kitchen, where he picked up Enemario and Riley, still stuffing his face just like at breakfast. The older woman who had been washing the floors on her hands and knees earlier beamed from ear to ear at Riley's excitement with her cooking.

"We're done here. Come on." Brady couldn't wait to get out of this place.

"But, Bones—" Riley stopped mid-sentence, realizing he'd made a slipup.

Enemario came in for the save. "Come on, bottom-less pit. He's tired and needs to rest. Can't you see?"

It was said for the benefit of whomever was surely listening.

CHAPTER 14

"**T**HAT IS TOTALLY fucked up!" shouted Riley.

Several of the team put their fingers to their lips to quiet him.

"I don't want to draw any attention to us, Riley." Brady said. "I'm just as pissed as you are, but that's not going to solve the problem. It is a huge mess, and he spent some time and energy setting this all up. We're on our own here. We don't have all the backup we used to have on the teams, so it is what it is. And, yeah, it's fucked."

Carter stood. "What's amazing to me is that none of these girls, when they run into something that doesn't work out for them, get news back to the ranch. You wonder what all these ladies think. People leave, and they never hear from them again. Or am I missing something?" Carter looked directly at Brady.

"It is just like what's happened in other countries. The girls hear what they want to hear. They think they're safe. This is what they do, and they do it so well. They trap them physically, psychologically, make it look like their life is going to be easy, and get their cooperation. In a way, it's kind of a cult, sort of brainwashing that goes on. Stockholm syndrome."

"Not to mention the fact that they have leverage," added John. "They have the kids. The woman who goes away knows that, if something goes bad, they'll never see their child again. It's pretty smart leverage, I'd say."

"Diabolical," said Riley.

"Here's the thing," Brady began. "It looks like Rojas isn't going to be back here for a couple of days. It's been a lot of work, and it was a good idea to come here, but now we know he's going to be in San Diego. I say we go get him from the Cinderella Slipper. We can get up there by tomorrow, cause a little drama, and yank him away from his payday. Because that's the reason he's there. Not to see the girls off, but to collect his money. I'd be willing to bet he doesn't trust anybody with that. Especially if it's a big payday."

There was general agreement this was to be their next course of action.

But Brady had another thing to add. "But we have to be careful not to outplay our hand. We can't draw attention to ourselves. Remember, we're not even supposed to be carrying weapons."

The team acknowledged him.

Without further delay, John cranked up the camper, and they headed back down the driveway, connected to the dirt "freeway," and drove all the way to the border.

THE TEAM TOOK turns driving the van. First thing in the morning, as dawn was breaking, they approached the outskirts of San Diego. Once again, they had slipped across the border, without much notice.

The Cinderella Slipper Hotel was grotesquely painted a bright pink color. Not a shade of flamingo or an attractive blushy color, but the color of a popular stomach ulcer remedy. On top of the revolving sign was a neon depiction of a glass slipper. It twinkled in the early sunlight of day.

As they approached the grounds, Brady noticed several warehouses nearby that had been abandoned, littered with old washing machines, cars without wheels, and other large pieces of garbage. There was no way this neighborhood was going through any kind of an urban renewal. Brady wondered what the young girls thought as they were driven here.

Avoiding the parking lots that looked more like a looter's paradise, they parked in the rest stop across the street from the hotel, because the hotel lot didn't accommodate a van as large as theirs. They also needed to have access for a quick getaway, in case it was necessary.

John set out cereal and cooked scramble eggs for them, while everyone washed their faces, checked their phones, and took turns taking a leak. A nice hot shower would make him feel whole and wash the stink of the ranch off his flesh, but he was going to have to wait a little while longer for that. Today, if they were perfect in their execution, they'd be hauling one Mr. Esquivel Rojas back to the Naval Base at Coronado, or another designated location. He was going to try the phone number for their benefactor one more time before they launched their next move.

"So we split up, search out the areas we designated last night. Riley, you're going see what you can find out from the security desk. John, you stay here with the vehicle. Carter and Enemario, you will find the location of the wedding ceremonies, if there are any."

"You mean you don't know if there's an actual wedding?" Riley wanted to know.

"At this point, anything goes. It could be just a *slam, bam, thank you, ma'am* exchange of dollars or an elaborate crucible event that they go through, kind of like a transfer of power. I have no fucking idea how he's doing this, but I do know he's probably gotten paid, and I'm guessing that he'll hang around long enough to make sure nobody's unhappy with their bargain."

"You mean if the Johns, the purchasers, won't be unhappy with the bargain." Carter once again appeared to harbor quite a bit of bitterness within his heart. Riley worried about that but was going to shelve it for now.

"Whatever we do, however we're able to impact this, I'm sure we'll be making the world a better place. Remember the goal is to take him alive. We may have to shoot him up with something, hurt him in some way, immobilize him. I don't care if he suffers; I just want him in this van at the end of the day. I want to turn him in, collect our money, and go home. I don't want to ever think about this guy again." Brady saw every single man agreed with him.

"We're close, and this is the time when things get all fucked up. This is when we plan one thing and then something else happens. So I'm going to need you all, even though we've not gotten the kind of sleep or we relaxation we intended, I need you all to be sharp. Don't assume everybody's doing their job, because there are a lot of moving parts here. No time for excuses, no time for blame. I don't want to hurt the girls, I certainly don't want to hurt innocent customers in the hotel, and I especially don't want anything to happen to any of you. I don't want to do anything that draws attention to us. We're going in for a quick extraction. The first part is to locate him, and the second is to get him out silently and quickly."

Enemario passed out the coms, and everybody did a mic test. John was going to monitor the equipment, and they retested their tapping protocol in case using their voice was not advisable. Riley passed out sidearms Brady had brought with him. They each were given two hundred dollars, and it was agreed they would take roughly an hour to complete their sweep of the hotel, bring back whatever intel they had, and reconvene in the van.

They slipped across the street one at a time, each man going directly to their designated spot.

Brady walked inside the lobby and was immediately struck with the odor of extremely strong aftershave. He glanced over the stained and lumpy overstuffed furniture that once might have looked nice, the old magazines and newspapers piled up on tables covered with paper cups and wrappers from fast food. Then he discovered the source of the aftershave avalanche, the young man behind the reception desk. Out of the side of his vision, he saw Enemario holding his nose, slip through a swinging door leading to the kitchen, and crossing himself before he disappeared.

The youth behind the desk was probably a college student, earning decent money while trying to pursue a degree. Brady imagined it would be an interesting job, for some.

"Can I help you, sir?" the man asked.

"I am looking for a wedding party. I believe there was a group gathering for a celebration?"

The man's eyes lit up. "Oh, yes. We had quite a party yesterday. I believe the guests will be leaving today."

"So is there... Did I miss the ceremony?" He squinted his eyes at the last minute, mimicking some kind of emotional pain.

The young attendant rolled his eyes. "You weren't the first person who asked about the wedding ceremonies. But honestly, I'm thinking there never was a ceremony."

Brady was not surprised. It was another curveball in a mission that wasn't turning out to be anything like what they thought it would be, but then they were hunting Esquivel Rojas, who seemed to have more than nine lives and possibly some high-level protection. Brady decided to chance bringing up the man's name.

"So I'm looking for Esquivel Rojas?"

The young man behind the desk straightened his pens, adjusted the login sheet lying on the desk in front of him, and quickly answered Brady. "I believe Mr. Rojas is in our Presidential Suite. I'm sorry, but I can't give you access. It's a dedicated elevator."

Brady had forgotten that about the penthouse. Years ago, several of his SEAL buddies had thrown one hell of a party there. What he remembered of it was not much.

"Okay, then I will wait for him to come downstairs. I have some important business to discuss with him. He asked me to meet him here." The attendant straightened his name badge, cleared his throat, and suggested a plan of action. "I can call him, but he asked not to be disturbed until past 10 o'clock. If you know Mr. Rojas, you know it's not a good idea to make him angry. I did that once yesterday, and I almost got fired."

"Good to know. No, I don't know Mr. Rojas. This is just business. We're not friends."

"Very well, we have a coffee shop, or there's a couple of diners down the road. I wouldn't recommend the food anywhere around here, but you could find some pretty good food carts, if you like Mexican food."

"I'm fine. I had breakfast already. So I can just take a seat here in the lobby then?"

"Yes, sir. Please. And help yourself to some complimentary coffee."

Brady sauntered over to the coffee and tea cart, took a whiff of what they called coffee, some dark black mixture that smelled like it had been percolated nearly twelve hours ago, and decided against tasting anything the hotel had to offer.

Brady surveyed the lobby, and years of his life crept back in as he did so. He didn't often think about those early days as a young SEAL, how it was exciting to wear his Trident or to be able to tell girls at the bar that he'd earned one. Eventually, he kept quiet about it.

The girls kept coming—that was never any problem. He had a good time in those days, being chased, being with a bunch of guys doing incredible things. People came up to him all the time and congratulated him on being on incredibly dangerous missions in foreign lands. But to Brady, he was having the time of his life. He felt he was the luckiest kid out there to find something he loved doing so well at such a young age. He looked at people in business, going to college, getting jobs, raising families, doing mundane things but not being really in love with anything. Brady wanted to live an emblazoned life full of color, turned up to the highest volume possible. He wanted to have fun, he wanted adventure, and he wanted to love deeply to help exorcise his demons.

It took him a while to learn everybody grows up with some childhood wounding. There's no such thing as a perfect, idyllic life, he mused. Over campfires in remote locations, he shared about his parents, his father's drinking, the death of his older brother, the girls he won and lost, and the way his mother always cried when he went away on deployments. It was just the patchwork, the stuff of life. They were the markers, the milestones of his time here on earth, not the real juice of being alive.

Brady had wanted to live full tilt. And if it took him out, so be it. He didn't want to be the guy just existing. He wanted to live like there was no tomorrow.

For a few years, the party times continued, but less and less, he hung around women. He stuck to his brothers, because those were the guys he could count on. And sure enough, most of them were flawed like he was, but they knew how to put their shit together and make it count when it was important. They knew what honor and keeping your word was all about, and they didn't use people. Well, they might borrow money and never pay it back, but it wasn't like they really used anybody. There were just some guys who spent money like water while others saved it.

Brady's deep love of his SEAL brothers supplanted all the joy that he used to have partying with the opposite sex. And more and more as the groups got together, Brady showed up alone.

Until he met Maggie.

Just by looking at him that first day they bumped into each other, Maggie dropped him on his ass.

He adjusted his seating angle, crossed his legs, and pulled his arms out to the sides, resting on the floppy couch.

What was it about Maggie that did that? She was as fearless as he was. She had a desire to live the same way. They didn't really make plans that year they spent together in San Diego. It was just assumed it was going to be like that from then on. He didn't have to convince her to stay with him, to love him, to be careful with his feelings, or to watch how she reacted to him even when she was tired, because when he came back from deployment, all he wanted to do was stay in bed with her. It was always five glorious days. Never four. Never six.

But Maggie wanted to do important things. She too was a force for good. And just like him, she would forego personal luxuries, postpone things they wanted so she could help someone out, give advice, and volunteer at the hospital when they were short-staffed. She was like that. She was a natural born healer. And she healed him from the affliction of ever wanting to be a normal man again.

Her loss created unspeakable pain. He couldn't remember crying since he was a child. But he had cried more after she was gone than he ever had before. His wounds kept bubbling back up to the surface. It was making him tired.

Maybe he'd made the wrong choice by going after Rojas. Maybe he should instead find something worthy to do, not eliminate somebody. Maybe he should cleave to the light side instead of the dark side. Maybe that's what was going on deep in his soul.

He liked his simple life, because it made it easier to cope with the day. Tate didn't ask much, and he was always there for him. That was about as complicated a relationship as he wanted right now. And, of course, if he needed more, well, he could always go look up one of his brothers.

But this caper had taught him he had to be doing things to really live. Not just checking out and waiting to die. And Brady realized that he'd spent the last while, especially the last twelve months, preparing to die. He'd forgotten the point of living.

He liked the idea of saving people who could not save themselves. Maybe his warrior days were not over yet. Maybe he should consider going back into the SEALs even though he was nearly forty years old. It had been done before. He'd known guys, talked to guys who did it. He just never saw that as something he could do. But maybe that's what he needed.

He also considered that maybe it was time to really grow up. Maggie was gone, and perhaps he should actively look for someone else. Someone who needed to be part of an intense partnership in every way. A physical, emotional, and spiritual connection. He did miss that part.

He'd been telling himself now for three years that it was gone forever. But this adventure had shown him there could be a door opening somewhere, and somebody might walk into that room and take that space. Even Maggie had told him that, when he found somebody else, she would disappear. And although it was still hard to imagine, he knew she was telling the truth. She was still guiding him, inspiring him, bringing him out of the dungeon of his own mind.

When he got back to Northern California, he was going to make some changes. Maybe he'd learn how to cook something other than game he'd shot, something he raised, and meat he butchered. He could take a cooking class, maybe learn how to garden professionally, or go see movies. If he certified Tate as a support animal, he could eat popcorn with him. And maybe, just maybe, while he was doing some of those other things, someone would walk in the doorway just like Maggie did that day in the hospital and would rock his world.

He remembered talking to one of his former commanding officers who had retired and had just lost his wife to cancer. He remembered this fellow in his seventies still thinking about being a husband. His wife had died, but he wasn't ready to stop being a partner. He wanted to care for someone.

Brady had thought he'd be relieved if he didn't have to take care of her, wash her, change her diapers, and never be far from her for very long because of her needs. But after she left, there was a huge hole in his world.

He had asked Brady that afternoon how he could go about finding another partner. Brady was shocked. It was the last thing in the world he expected his former CO to say.

"I don't know. Is there some place you can go and find them? You would certainly know better than I."

"I could go to the library, I could wander up and down the grocery aisles, I could sit in the park and read, I could take my dog to obedience class. I just don't know what to do. Brady, I've always been told we aren't the ones that make the decisions. The women choose us."

Brady listened to him and realized he was right.

"Goddamn it, Bill, you're a wise old fart. I never thought of it that way."

"So how do you get a woman to fall in love with you, Brady? How do I get a good woman to choose me?"

Brady sat back that day, looked at the ceiling, and then glanced outside. In the man's garden, he maintained his former wife's roses, trimming, deadheading, and fertilizing them with great care just like he always had when she was sick and convalescing. Her bed looked out at that rose garden. Every day, he clipped one perfect rose and placed it by her head on the bedside table.

As he was studying the beautiful flowers, a butterfly landed on one of them, flapped its spotted yellow wings back and forth, and walked with black spindly legs clutching the rich red, velvety rose petals. And then just as quickly as it landed, it flew off.

He turned to his former commanding officer and said, "It's the same way, Bill, that you get a butterfly to land on you. You sit there, you become like a rose, and she just comes. She finds you. You wait for her to find you."

CHAPTER 15

O NE BY ONE, Brady watched as his team passed by him in the lobby on the way to their van. It had only been thirty-five minutes. Not the hour he had allotted them, but it was their way of showing him that something urgently needed to be shared.

He was the last to join them, closing the door to the little vehicle behind him.

"What have we got?"

"First," Riley began, "I have to say that I think we should make our move now. I don't want to wait for any more people to wake up or arrive. If anybody recognizes this van or us or starts asking questions, they're going to pull in their security, and we're going to have a lot rougher time. I've checked with the security manager, but I don't trust him. It would be just like him to alert Rojas. I mean, his salary probably depends on it."

Several others agreed audibly.

"Okay, I'll buy that. That's a good point, and we should escalate this and move quickly. What else do we need to know before we begin? Anybody see any traps, anything that looks suspicious, anybody lying in wait for us that you can detect?"

Carter fidgeted, tapping his fingers on his knee. "I don't think they got anything sophisticated at all set up. Rojas thinks he's about to get away scot-free. He's just come in to a whole lot of money, and he's going to enjoy himself for a day. It's stupid, and maybe somebody will suggest otherwise, but I think he's allowing himself just a few minutes of breathing room, and—"

Enemario interrupted him "He has protection. I understand from talking to the head housekeeper that, when he comes here, he entertains several local police and San Diego sheriffs. He lets them stay with the girls for free."

That got Brady's attention as well.

"So the penthouse is not accessible from below."

Enemario held up a passkey. "Housekeeping has to clean. They have access. I borrowed it."

"Excellent. Okay. So we already packed our bags last night and checked it this morning. Right?"

"Roger that," several members said.

Enemario added, "I made sure I brought something not too explosive. Enough for a distraction but nothing that will get the fire department called."

"Good." Brady checked his watch. "We should get out of here and head up that elevator. I want Riley and John to stay downstairs in the lobby, guarding the entrance. Is there an escape from the third floor?"

Enemario shook his head, "No. There is a stairwell in the ceiling in the hallway that goes to the roof. In case of a fire, they evacuate by helicopter on top."

Brady nodded. "Good to know. If we trap them in the elevator, we've got him in case he slips by when we do the breach, okay?"

Everyone was in.

"Carter, I want you outside. I'd like you to claim that little outhouse or whatever the hell it is. Take your long gun and focus it on the entrance. You hear a whole bunch of commotion, and Esquivel exits through the front door, you pop him. Not lethal, but you put him down."

"Roger that, sir. I'm on my way." Carter took his duty bag, slung it over his shoulder, and quietly ran for the shed.

"He'll tell us when he's in position. That's the signal to go, so get your gear right now. Check everything you need to check. Make sure you have not left behind something you're going to need. Bring your knives as well, but make sure you have your SIG Sauer."

Brady heard the "in position" message on his phone.

"We're go, gentlemen."

Brady took the lead with Enemario right behind him. They kept their weapons stowed. After they entered the lobby, John and Riley sealed the front door, locking the mechanism. Enemario pushed the elevator button to the penthouse, which got the attention of the desk clerk.

"You're going to want to stand down, sir, and just let them have their way. If you stay calm, everything will be okay, and you won't get hurt," Riley said to him.

The young man's eyes nearly popped out of his head. "What are you doing? Mr. Rojas is up there. That's Esquivel Rojas."

"I'm aware of who the gentleman is. Is he alone?"

"He has a woman. He may have security up there, but I did not see anybody last night, and I've been here all morning. I would say no."

"Okay. I'm going to take you to your office, and we're going to have a calm little chat." Just as Riley took the desk clerk to his office to secure him, the doors to the elevator opened, and Enemario and Brady stepped inside, nodding to John. John scanned the front and gave him the thumbs-up just before the doors closed.

It took just a few seconds to reach the top floor. Enemario had disabled the bell on his way, and he allowed the doors to close behind them and return to the lobby. There were only two doorways for the entire top floor. One led outside to a garden area accessible only from the penthouse. It's glass window indicated the patio was empty. The other door had number 6900.

Brady held up his fingers and pointed to the door latch. Enemario presented the passkey, and there was a loud click as the lock receded. They waited several seconds, standing at the sides in case someone was alerted on the inside. Hearing nothing, Enemario turned the handle and slowly opened the door. Music was playing very faintly. The drapes were pulled, and wine glasses and plates littered the living room, spilling onto the countertops in the kitchen. Clearly, a small gathering had occurred last night.

Brady knew from past experience that this penthouse was rather small. There was only one bedroom, but it did have its own huge bathroom and laundry facility. It also had a pantry off the kitchen for guests to hire catering staff. The door to the bedroom was ajar, and it was completely black.

The sunlight cascading into the living room would expose them once they opened the door fully, since the room was in darkness and they were in light. Brady took out his flashlight, turned it on, and tucked it in his shirt pocket. With both hands on his SIG Sauer, he led the two of them into the bedroom. There were two bodies on the bed. One was obviously a woman's backside and spine, and she was lying on top of a man. The man was snoring. They both appeared to be asleep.

Brady held his SIG with one hand and motioned to Enemario to cover him. He flashed the light in the gentleman's eyes.

He was rewarded when he saw the torso of Esquivel Rojas rise and then scramble off the bed, pressing his back to the wall.

"Son of a bitch. You won't get away with this. I didn't think anyone was so stupid," Rojas said. The girl began to scream, and Enemario grabbed her from behind, pinched her neck, and eased her to the floor.

"You're coming with us, Rojas." Brady wasn't there to reason with him, wasn't there to talk to him or explain anything. This was a quick snatch and grab.

Something squawked in his ear, but he couldn't make it out. Esquivel briefly glanced down at the bedside table, and Brady noticed a revolver tucked under a book there. Brady reached for it and handed it to Enemario, who tucked it in his pants. Rojas stood in his bare feet, his pajama bottoms sagging a bit beneath his belly, and was shirtless.

"We're going now."

"I have to get my shoes."

"No can do," Enemario said.

Brady grabbed Rojas' right and left arms, placing them together and securing them with a zip tie behind his back. He grabbed his shoulder so hard Rojas winced.

"Okay, asshole, we're going for a ride."

Aiming his SIG at the back of Rojas's head, he followed Enemario who was standing by the elevator after calling for it. As the doors opened, Enemario quickly aimed for any possible intruder and found it empty. The three of them entered, and Enemario pushed the button for the floor to the lobby.

"You are a dead man. You don't know anything about this."

"I know enough to grab you."

As the doors opened, they were greeted by seven police and one Naval officer with their guns drawn and aimed directly at Brady.

Brady's heart sank as he looked into the eyes of Lieutenant Commander Roland Stanley.

"At ease, gentlemen. Drop your weapons. Release the hostage."

Brady refused to comply. Enemario had started to lower his weapon but then left his hands in position.

"I would love to shoot you in the head, you asshole, you misfit. I've waited for years, so don't think I won't do it."

Without regard to his own safety, Lieutenant Commander Roland Stanley walked directly toward Brady and pointed his police special in the middle of his forehead. "I said drop it."

Brady stepped back and held his SIG to the side. One of the officers picked it up, grabbing Enemario's as well. Stanley pointed to the gun stuffed in Enemario's belt, and the policeman removed it.

Esquivel Rojas turned and gave Brady a cheesy grin. "I told you, you'll never get away with it. There wasn't a chance in hell I was going to be captured on American soil. I don't think you understand how important I am to your government."

"That's enough, Rojas," shouted Stanley. "Keep your trap shut."

"Then I will go upstairs and get my clothes. Would one of you officers like to accompany me?"

Esquivel held out his hand to Enemario. "The key, please?"

Enemario laid the brass passkey in the middle of his palm. He didn't take his eyes off the man, however. Brady noticed Enemario didn't appear to have an ounce of fear.

As Rojas unceremoniously slipped across the lobby in his striped pajama bottoms, his feet padding on the carpet, Stanley called after him. "I want you back down here in five minutes. Officer Craig? See to it that he doesn't use his cell phone, please?"

"You got it."

Before they reached the elevator, Stanley reconsidered. "Someone else go with him too." Instantly, one of the Naval security patrol ran after the two of them, catching up just before the doors closed.

Stanley motioned for Brady and Enemario to take seats in the lobby. He had one of the other San Diego sheriffs secure their wrists and their ankles. Riley was led into the lobby at gunpoint from the manager's office and was instructed to sit across from Brady. John had been handcuffed to a pillar by the front door. He remained standing.

They didn't appear to have found the sniper outside, who could hear everything Brady said.

"So I want to know how come you're stopping me from apprehending this criminal. Do you know what he does for a living?"

Stanley paced back and forth in front of Brady, preening like a peacock. Finally, he stopped, turned to him, and said, "Of course I know. That's why I'm here. Mr. Rojas is an asset. We have been very successful in bringing down one of the largest cartels in Baja, California recently, and we are about to finish the last strike to put the nail in the coffin so that this family will never rise again. We could not have done that without Rojas. Tons of narcotics will now be dumped into the ocean instead of injected into the veins of our youth. I consider that a win-win."

"At the cost of women and children sold into slavery and stolen from their families, to become sex objects for perverts." Brady knew Stanley must understand what Rojas was involved in but was turning a blind eye. "You honestly think you can deal with somebody who does that to women and children? Don't you have any compassion, Stanley? You have a wife and children. What would happen if a guy like that got hold of them? Have you ever considered that?"

"Well, first of all, I keep my wife safe." Stanley peered into Brady's soul with the cool gray eyes of a snake. He had not an ounce of compassion. The message was clear. Brady was responsible for Maggie's death.

Brady seethed, stood up, and pushed himself into Stanley's body. Willing to take a bullet to crush this man who had stopped him once from preserving whatever decency was left in his life, from saving Maggie. He'd interfered at that very important juncture of the mission and was interfering again today.

Stanley was light on his feet, and because he did not fall, Brady remained standing as well. He soon had two arms around him, pushing him back into the couch. Stanley straightened his uniform as his cell phone rang.

"Bring him down now." Stanley listened and then repeated himself. "I said, bring him down. I don't care who he's called. You bring him down right now." He waited again and then gave his order a third time.

"Then you bring them both down please."

Exasperated, he said something under his breath, shaking his head from side to side.

"So what happens now, Stanley?"

"Well, I think the Navy is going to lock you up until we work out the jurisdictional issues, since you are now my prisoner, interfering with my operation. In the long run, the court system will find you an attractive target, and as they so expertly do, they'll drain your bank account of every penny you own, taking your beloved property and turning you into the inmate that you really always have been."

Brady kept quiet about his orders. And he wasn't going to volunteer that he had a possibility of protection.

Rojas and his young companion were fully dressed and joined them in the lobby. "I would like to leave now."

Stanley, who was about six inches taller than Rojas, peered down at him like he was a bug. "You'll have to remain here just a little while longer, Esquivel. I apologize. We have some paperwork, and I need to verify that it is protocol to release you. But ultimately, not to worry, you will be leaving soon."

Cocky from the information he'd received, Esquivel decided to dig into Brady a little further. "How in the world did you think you could get me, and why did you think it was going to be a good idea?"

"I wondered the same, Brady. You just came up with this on your own?" Stanley asked.

"I have been thinking of nothing else for the past three years, ever since he murdered my Maggie."

There it was. He'd said it, finally. Admitted to the whole fucking room the one thing that had haunted him, the one thing that hurt him so badly he could hardly stand it every time he thought of it. Instead of acknowledging, Rojas broke out in a huge belly laugh.

"You are so dumb, Brady. So impossibly dumb. You see, what I do will ultimately last forever. It's the oldest profession in the world, and it will still exist two thousand years from now. You can't stop this. People want to better themselves, and they will do just about anything to get there."

"I will never give up. I will have my revenge," Brady said defiantly.

Esquivel turned to his companion. "Do you have your certificate?"

"Sí, sí. Let me look." She sat down and began rummaging through a large purse. She extracted a Manila envelope, opened the clasp, and slipped out a piece of paper, handing it to Esquivel Rojas.

Mr. Rojas held the paper in front of Brady and said, "Read it. Read her certificate."

Brady was looking at the heading on the certificate,

which said Evidence of Live Birth. Enemario and Riley were reading along with him, Riley leaning over his shoulder to do so.

"So she's had a baby. What does that matter? Did you sell her baby? Is that what you're telling everybody you're so proud of, Rojas?"

"Read the signature of the attending physician."

Brady's eyes scanned the baby's name and the April date, meaning it was six months prior to today. He kept scanning until he came to the bottom of the page where there was a beautifully scrawled signature. He recognized the penmanship.

Maggie May.

CHAPTER 16

BRADY WAS IN Hell itself. Fires, huge plumes of red danced all around him. He heard people crying. Someone was laughing at the demise of the world. It was all being shredded. He could not take his eyes off the signature on the certificate. The significance of what he was looking at could not be comprehended. It was like he needed to get over the wall to safety, but he didn't have a ladder and the wall was too high. Even if he jumped, he couldn't keep his footing.

He felt the sweat rolling down the middle of his spine and across his forehead. Drips of perspiration landed on his shirt. The huge wet semi-circles under his arms did not soothe him. He could not make his eyes move.

Riley came up behind him and shook him by the shoulders, making Brady lose focus. He knew he was still in Hell, but Hell was down a long dark tunnel, a smooth shot to oblivion. He sought a quick death. He sought an end to the pain.

"No, no, Brady, hang in there. This is not you. Come on," Riley was saying.

Brady saw a scuff mark on the coffee table in front of him. It was like a Nike swoosh, odd looking thing, but he found he had to focus on it.

"Get me some water, quick!" Riley's voice barked. People in front of him bumped into each other. Someone released Brady, unbuttoning his shirt.

"He's cold and clammy. He's going into shock." Brady recognized that person who was a medic, a medic he had trained. Someone else was checking his blood pressure. He couldn't hear what was being said, because he had great big earmuffs covering his ears. He began shivering.

Everything he thought about the last three years was a lie. It was not reality. It felt like his brain had split into two, and half of it was dead. The other half struggled to make everything work. His heart was racing.

He examined the faces in front of him—shocked faces, some worried faces. He saw one face smiling at him. He knew that face. He hated that face.

Riley was shaking his shoulders again. Somebody slapped his cheeks. Brady's swift right hand reached up, grabbed that person's forearm, and twisted it until he heard it crack. A scream pierced the room. He looked down at his lap and saw the slits that dug into his flesh. He'd broken the zip ties all by himself. But it cut him. And just like if a razor ran across his veins, his blood covered his thighs and soaked into the couch. He could even feel it running down the backs of his legs. He still couldn't move.

His vision was rimmed in a shiny black circle. The circle kept getting smaller and smaller. If he waited long enough, if he just waited until that circle disappeared completely, he would float into nothingness, that place of no pain. He would vanish into nothing, like Maggie did. Maggie faded into the pillow all the time. Maggie was gone. But Maggie was still here? Had he heard that somewhere?

He frowned, looked up at one worried face, and asked the question, "Where am I? Where's Tate? Did somebody catch Tate?"

Behind him, someone was in pain. Someone else was swearing. Another person gave instructions.

"Here, Brady. Drink this water please."

Riley was right there next to him, holding the clear plastic cup. Brady couldn't lift his hand. He wanted to. So he bent his head, leaned onto the water cup, and slurped several cool sips. It tasted wonderful. Then something in his stomach began to roll around as the cold water doused the flames, chased away the demons. It made him cold, and he started to shiver again.

"John? What do I do now?"

Riley was asking for advice from John. John was the medic that Brady trained. He was also in pain. In between sobs and cries of pain, John ordered them to call 911. "He has to get to a hospital and be seen. It could be a heart attack."

Brady suddenly turned his head. He could see John lying on the floor holding his forearm. Someone was trying to immobilize him, making a sling out of a piece of his shirt. Brady stared at the fractured forearm.

"I did that. John, I am so sorry."

"Ah, it's just a little accident," Riley tried to reassure him. "Here, Brady. Pay no attention. Drink some more water. You feel better?"

"Where's Tate?" he heard himself say. "Where's Maggie?" The whistle in the back of his brain continued to scream and then slowly began to fade.

John shouted out to him, "Breathe, Brady. Take a deep breath and lean over. Breathe."

"John. I hurt you, John."

"Yes, you did that, Brady. Yep, welcome back. Come back to us, Bones."

It was Riley, Riley who was shaking his shoulders and moving his upper torso. His legs were warm, and then he saw the blood again.

"This is my blood?"

The reaction from the crowd standing around him was swift. People crashed into each other. There was lots of yelling. A gun went off. Someone said, "Don't let Rojas get out of here. Find him!"

Riley was speaking to his ear, whispering, encouraging him to come back.

He liked hearing from his friend, his reassuring words. He couldn't respond except to say, "Good."

Vehicles pulled up to the lobby area. Several armed men arrived, holding the little conclave at bay. Brady looked up and saw Stanley staring down at him in disbelief.

He started to say something. "How—"

Rojas was tied, both hands and feet, yelling and objecting to being confined. He was lifted by his arm pits by two heavily armed guards and left the lobby area, his screams following him until Brady heard the slam of a door.

A short, attractive woman suddenly appeared, knelt in front of him, and placed her palms on his hands. He noticed the edges of her shirt began to accept his blood.

"Careful," he whispered.

She smiled. It was good to see a smile. "Brady, we got him. You did it. You and your team did it."

He recognized her voice as being the one from the phone call. All of a sudden, things started to fit into place. Tate wasn't here, because he was back in Northern California. Maggie was dead, but maybe she wasn't. Rojas was gone, because he was the mission. John had something wrong with his arm, something he did. And his best friends surrounded him.

She stood up, leaned over, and shook his right shoulder. "Brady, words cannot express how grateful we are to you. I am going to leave now, but we will be talking again very soon." She turned.

"Who are you?" Brady asked to her back.

"My name is not important. I'm going to give you some time to collect your thoughts. And then we will have a private conversation. I want you to know that the mission was accomplished. All you need to do now is to just get well, heal yourself. You did it. You all did it." She looked at Riley, Enemario, and John. She nodded to Carter. "I have to say, I am so impressed."

Roland Stanley was standing tall and stiff immediately behind her. She wheeled around to face him, and the fact that he was towering over her, almost gloating, did not affect her demeanor one bit. Brady saw in her something of Maggie. She spoke three quick sentences, telling him that he was going to jail and would be brought up on charges for his participation in aiding and abetting a known sex trafficker, prostitution, and the sale of drugs. His entire staff would join him in prison someday. She promised she would have him prosecuted to the fullest extent of the law.

When she turned around to face Brady again, Roland's ashen face began to shrivel, and he began to sob uncontrollably. "Get him out of my sight!" Several seconds later, it was done.

She addressed him again, her voice softening. "Brady, you are going to have to go to the hospital. I will arrange for a private room for you. I want you to say nothing." She looked at the other men in his team. "None of you say anything."

Carter was the first to say, "Yes ma'am."

"You take good care of this hero." She stared until all of them were nodding—even Brady.

Then he remembered Maggie. He looked up at this strange woman, asking, "Maggie. They told me she's alive. Tell me the truth."

The young woman knelt again and once more placed her palms over the tops of Brady's hands. As she began to speak, an ambulance with lights and siren blasting rolled up to the front door.

"I only have two seconds here, but she is safe and you will get to see her. That's all you need to know. Well done." She stood up and faded into the crowd just like Brady imagined. She was gone just like Maggie.

Two uniformed orderlies picked Brady up and placed him on a stretcher. He fought them, trying to grab one of their forearms. His team rushed to the aid of the attendant, and he heard Riley shouting, "No, no, no. You get your hand out of there. Brady, stop it, let go!" Brady felt his fingers loosen. He looked up at Riley and said, "I don't want to hurt anybody anymore."

"That makes two of us, big guy," Riley returned. "Just try to relax. These guys will take care of everything."

The walls of the lobby closed in on him. He shut his eyes. He heard noises for several minutes, and then he heard the ocean. He saw the beach in San Diego, where they used to walk at night. He let the warmth from the moon cover his body and shine on her long copper locks. He wondered if it was a dream or if he'd just woken up from another nightmare. Which scene was real and which one was the dream?

But he knew he had to sleep.

CHAPTER 17

WHEN BRADY OPENED his eyes, the light was blinding. He heard scuffling about his hospital bed, aware of where he was, but not sure who was in the room with him. As his eyes got accustomed to the brightness, he saw on Enemario, John, Riley, and Carter standing around the foot of the bed. He examined his arms, noting the bandages covering his wrists, and moved his toes and legs. He grinned up at them.

"So you guys might've thought I was out of it, but I heard some things." He squinted. "Very revealing. You should be careful when you're standing around somebody you think is unconscious."

The men glanced amongst themselves and then, one by one, disputed his claim.

"Enemario, I heard you say that I was going crazy."

"Well, boss, you were saying some crazy shit. You were talking about Tate, and you know, I thought they should give you something to be quiet."

"Because it made you nervous. I made you nervous," Brady argued.

Enemario had no defense, so he shrugged.

Riley came to Enemario's defense. "In all fairness, Brady, he's right about what you were talking about. And would you look at your hands, your wrists?"

Brady held up his hands and paid more attention to the bandages. "Did I try to end my life?"

John laughed and showed him his sling. "No, but you tried to rip my arm off. That was freaky, Brady."

"Yeah, I know. I'll have to make it up to you guys when I'm out of here. I'm going to do a big barbecue up there, and we're going to party all night long under the stars."

Are these my words? Did I just do that?

Riley gave him a respectful smile. "You just get yourself well. The barbecue can wait. But when you're ready, we're going to party like there was no tomorrow. So understand, a promise is a promise, right?"

Brady nodded, and then tears filled his eyes and ran down his cheeks. Enemario was first to hand him a wad of Kleenex. "Boss, you don't need to cry for John. He's tough."

Everyone laughed.

Brady blotted his eyes. "Yeah, but sometimes I'm not. I'm sorry what I put you through."

Carter was next to tease him. "You sure did scare

the hell out of me. I got to admit I thought you was totally scrambled. I thought to myself, okay, it's straightjacket time. They're never going to let him out of the hospital. Brady's fried."

"Thank you. I'll remember that, as you age."

Everybody laughed again.

Brady knew that Esquivel Rojas had been taken away by the mysterious woman who met them that day. He asked if anybody had had a chance to talk to her.

"No, Brady she took off. But Rojas wasn't the only one arrested. They also got Stanley. And good riddance, I say. Navy's got a black eye for that one," added Carter. "You know how I feel about that slimeball."

"Amen to that, fellas," said Brady.

"We were going to fly Tate down here so he could be with you while you were convalescing, but since we haven't gotten paid yet, none of us could afford the ticket," added John.

The joke went over well with the group, but Brady knew it was a call to action.

"It feels good to laugh," he said, wiping his eyes again. "I'll make sure you guys get paid right away."

"We'll have those conversations just as soon as you're out of here, okay? In the meantime, don't stress about it. John's all fired up to buy himself a new truck and a lost weekend," said Riley.

"I can't wait to go home myself," said Brady. Then he got serious. "I guess the last thing I've got to ask you guys about is Maggie. Was I hallucinating or is she alive?"

Enemario smirked then covered his mouth with his hand. "That's above my pay grade. I'm going to let other people explain that to you. But from what I understand, she agreed to help him for a limited time, expecting he would let her go. But I'll let you discuss it with her."

Brady was beginning to tear up again. "I'm not sure when I'm going to be ready for that. I'm just glad we all made it out of there safe."

Carter hung his head, "You just go with the flow, Brady. Get the facts first. The rest will reveal itself in time."

"You know something I don't?" he asked them.

"You heard the lady, Brady. Our lips are sealed. She'll arrange your meeting when you're ready," said Riley.

"I can't wait to get you that money. You guys earned it, every penny."

OVER THE NEXT several days, Brady was bored sitting in bed, and even when he was allowed to walk up and down the hallway, he still longed to be free of the tubes, the hospital, and the constant waking him up. The, he was told he had a visitor. He was not surprised when the mysterious woman who showed up at the Cinderella Slipper Hotel that night was standing in front of his bed.

"I guess you're still not going to tell me your name, am I right about that?"

"You're entitled to it, but no, that's not happening anytime soon. Brady, what I will tell you is, just like in any company, the business of running a country is made up of all sorts of factions, and to be honest with you, you wouldn't want it any other way. Sometimes two or more factions begin warring against each other, and it happens when they stop talking, trusting each other. Then you have one side trying to impose its will on the other. You're think I work for the government, and you would be wrong. I work for the American people."

"Okay. Is there a point to this, or is it a long way of just telling me to bug off?"

"You're unusually funny for having survived this whole ordeal."

"On the teams, we call it gallows humor."

"I understand. Brady, we want to protect what we all hold dear, which is our freedoms. And our history has not been perfect. We've followed a fragile path to come to where we are today. But it became necessary for us to intercede in a situation we discovered. Roland

Stanley was using Esquivel Rojas just as much as Esquivel Rojas was using him and all the women and children he abused. It was the perfect storm of two big egos, one cooking up an organization and one protecting the activator of the organization. That infection was going to spread."

"That part I understood perfectly."

She smiled. He liked it when she did that. "While confidential informants help us solve half of the problems that we have, there comes a time when the operation just doesn't make sense anymore. Or the sacrifices are too great or it's just too much of a risk. Stanley stepped over the line, and because you and some of the members of your team incurred his wrath years ago, you seemed like the perfect fit, the perfect candidates for this job. I did not know until eight days ago that Maggie was still alive. And, Brady, if I'd known that, I'm not sure I would have asked for your help. We have some issues with that, and I can't promise you one hundred percent how it'll play out, but we are trying to convince two federal judges that Maggie was brainwashed, leveraged, and compromised into doing things she would not normally do. But I have to tell you, it may be a long road."

"I'm not sure I'm ready to see her."

"I understand. I really do. And I don't want to impose my will on anybody, but in this case, circumstances make it so I think the two of you should talk. I would like you to hear from her what happened and how it happened. It's a very compelling story, Brady."

"You've been very straight with me. I still don't understand why you have to remain anonymous, but I will accept your challenge."

"Well, I'm glad you recognize that, because not many people ever meet me. I do my work behind the scenes. I'm a non-person. I don't want attention. I just want things to get better. I ask myself all the time, is this going to bring people together or is it going to tear them apart? Is it going to make it so the boats row in the same direction or they keep going around and round in circles and never travel anywhere? You may be familiar with those concepts, because I believe it was part of your training as a SEAL."

"It was."

"You took on this job agreeing to do it for one million, Brady. You accomplished the goal, and you enlisted the support of men you could count on. It was not pretty. It was full of flaws, but it worked. I'm authorized to tell you that we have agreed to double the fee. This'll be done later on today, and your cohorts, well, I hope they appreciate it. Because this never happens."

"I didn't do it for the money. I did it for revenge."

"That is why, Brady, you need to have a discussion with Maggie."

"Just like that?"

"Let me ask you this. Do you wonder if she's a criminal?"

"I wonder if I can trust her, yes. I loved her. But seeing her name on that certificate, it almost made her responsible for it. I don't understand why she would choose to willingly work with a murderer like that."

"Very well. I note your objection. I'm just asking you to reconsider. You may never be ready to face it, but when you are, the phone number in your mobile will now work, and you can leave a message on a machine. I feel like I owe it to you to remain accessible, because this part of my job is incomplete. You've earned your money, yes, but in the process, you've lost something even greater. I hold some responsibility for that."

She stood.

"You're leaving?"

"Got another situation I need to get up and running. There's always something. I'd love to hang around you guys, but I can't."

"Thanks for the personal visit then."

"We may not talk, but you can tell me things. On the machine."

"Does that mean we have a relationship?" Brady

looked up at her and saw he made her blush.

"Well, this is good-bye for now. No, I'm not going to answer that question, Brady, because you already know the answer. You take good care of yourself and Tate. Go heal. That's what I want you to do."

"Fine. I will do that. And I appreciate it."

There was something else Brady wanted to say, but he couldn't put his finger on it. As he watched her leave his room, he remembered. He had promised himself to do things out of goodness, to remain a force for good, rather than to live in the state of revenge. He'd been baptized in a fire of his own making. This was going to be a real test of his courage, to see how well he could put his life back together again.

As he looked at all the things he needed to do, the paths he needed to follow, every single one of them passed by Maggie's doorway. He was not quite ready, but he was planning to be.

CHAPTER 18

B RADY WAS GIVEN the choice to remain in San Diego for another week, just to give himself some rest and care and perhaps a little reunification with some of his buddies from SEAL Team 5, the team he had detached from several years ago. While the offer was generous and tempting, Brady wanted to go home.

Of course, he didn't want to say he missed his dog. That wouldn't appear to be very manly, but Tate was a big part of his decision. And damn it, if he couldn't do the things he really needed to do and missed the most, what was the point of hanging around a bunch of guys who were doing things he used to do? He'd be sitting on the sidelines, experiencing his age and the fact he probably would never be able to do it again. So as tempting as a week or two in a rented cottage at the beach was, he told them that, at this point in his development, he was not interested. He needed to get back to his real life, his gardens, and his home. He was sure there was a lot of work that would need to be done.

He was prepared to find the worst—that his gardens had been overrun with animals and his grow had disappeared—but it was good work, work that made him happy. Plus, people would leave him alone there.

So he accepted Enemario's offer to drive him from his home in San Diego up to Sonoma County. Everyone else had gone back to their respective towns. He told the organization that, at some future point, he might take them up on the little cottage at the beach. And he appreciated the offer. He wanted them to know it just wasn't what he needed.

As they drove up I-5, he remembered Enemario's metal flake stretch Hummer always attracted attention wherever he drove it. And Brady wasn't used to that. Other drivers honked, and some of them gave them a thumbs-up. A few gave them the finger. Enemario was unabashed in his love of the United States, his back bumper being filled with American flags stickers from many of the special forces he had worked with in the past, his old PD badge, and "save the whales" for good measure.

"I forgot you had that on there," said Brady.

"Ah, the girls like it. I don't want them thinking I'm just some crazy guy, that if they get in an accident or something, I'm going to pull out a gun and shoot them.

I got enough of the other kind of stickers all over it, and to be honest with you, most people are okay with it. But I had to put that on there. A friend of mine's daughter wanted to put a unicorn on there too, but I stopped that."

Brady was always amazed at how open-minded and easy to be with Enemario was. He wasn't born with a silver spoon in his mouth but came from a very loving and tight family. Brady envied that in the man.

As they bumped along the highway, several hours into their trip, they passed by the Fresno and Selma turnoffs. They observed the drying orchards to one side, while orchards on the other side of the freeway were green and lush. For sale signs were everywhere as ranches transferred ownership. New people came in to do what perhaps the old farmers couldn't achieve.

It was sad seeing the changes, but Brady understood the world was changing every day. And not always for the good, either. But he had no background or knowledge in real farmers' issues, so he didn't dwell on what he saw. He did know he preferred the lush green valley of his little parcel of Heaven, north of Healdsburg, over the dry, brown fallowness of the failed fields and orchards.

Things became more and more familiar to him as they completed their tenth hour, not counting their rest stops and meal breaks. He was getting more and more excited to see his patch. He had hoped he'd be able to see it in sunlight, but this time of year, it fell dark earlier, and without daylight savings kicking in, it was going to be pitch black when he arrived.

But he didn't mind. He wanted to be home.

They turned off the highway and slipped through downtown Healdsburg until they encountered the country roads going north to Brady's ranch. Downtown looked about the same with the bevy of tourists screwing around the benches and sidewalks, eating ice cream cones, sipping on glasses of wine out on the verandas at the many restaurants downtown, and a band playing in the rotunda of the square. Some older hippie chicks were dancing, their long hair flowing, showing off the fact that they still grooved in their sixties and seventies or perhaps beyond.

That would always be part of the California, especially Northern California, lifestyle.

It brought a smile to Brady's lips. "I guess, someday, I'll be gray-haired with a long ponytail, and I'll do that too. What do you think, Enemario?"

"Shit, Brady, you're not an old man. You're not even forty yet. What the fuck are you thinking?"

"I'm thinking that I'm getting old. That's all. I mean, heart attack? In danger of a stroke? Now I got to be careful. They've got me on medicines I never used to have to take."

"Be glad you got some good help. Just be glad you're alive, Brady. You've got more than half your life left. You're going to live to be over a hundred. I know it."

"Maybe you're right. Maybe this trip has taught me that. I used to think it would be better to die in the heat of battle. And I'm not saying this because I want to die, Enemario, please understand me."

"Oh, thank God. You had me scared there for a while. Don't think about that too much. You know what they say. If you do, then the undertaker comes and gets you in your sleep. You stop thinking and dreaming about that."

"No, I don't. You don't understand. I've developed a new perspective about what I want to do. I don't know what it is yet, but I'd like to do something good, because God knows, we sure did kill a bunch of people, captured people, and destroyed buildings and schools trying to get the bad guys. Now, I'd like to do something else. It's really calling me."

Enemario was silent for several minutes. Brady wasn't sure he was entirely accepting his words.

"Well, Brady, as long as it doesn't involve going down to Baja California to go get a bad guy or raid a camp somewhere where bad guys want to kill us or jumping out of an airplane into a snake-infested jungle, I'll do that with you. You just let me know. I mean, I owe you. I earned a lot of money for just a couple of weeks' worth of work. It was good work, and we helped a lot of people. At the same time, Brady, you have to understand we can't help everybody."

"I get you. No worries there. Yeah, I'd like to stay more in touch. I'd like to have you guys come up and go hunting with me. Maybe we'll do some project together. You know, give back somehow. I'd like for people, when they thank me for my service, to thank me for doing something good besides death and destruction?"

"But, Brady, somebody has to do it."

"Oh, I completely agree. I'm not saying we don't. It's just my turn to do something else. Does that make sense?"

"Absolutely. And Tate will be most happy if you stay close to home a lot more. From what Riley has told me, he looks out the front door every morning to see if you're going to come get him. Riley said he never gave up hope. He always knew you would come."

Brady was touched. "I didn't know that. Thank you."

Just as they entered Brady's bridge, the automatic gate opened, and Brady felt the relaxation of knowing that he was finally home. They turned the corner as the gate closed behind them, several hundred feet from the front door. Even though Tate may not have remembered Enemario's truck, he surely recognized Brady sitting in the passenger seat, because that dog barreled from the front porch and ran full tilt to meet them halfway.

Enemario came to a screeching halt, the truck skidding about four feet in the dirt driveway. Brady was out the door before he fully stopped.

Tate's body slammed Brady so hard they both fell back and rolled in the dirt. He wouldn't allow Brady to protect his head and face, jumping all over him, licking him, and dancing on his belly. Brady had never seen Tate so excited.

A small contingent sat on the porch, clapping and laughing at Tate's reaction. Tate jumped off Brady, barked at them as if telling them to shut up, and then came back to his master. Still in seated position, Brady asked Tate to sit, which he did dutifully, and then he began to rub his ears and talk to him.

"Tate, I missed you. I understand you've been doing good work up there at Riley's place, and I'm glad you didn't bite the kids. That I was worried about."

Tate panted. His heart was still racing, and when Brady finished his sentence, he leaned over and licked his face again.

"I know you know what I'm saying. Now, killing the rooster, that's a different story. He still was somebody's pet, and you shouldn't have done that."

Tate angled his head and didn't lick Brady's face this time.

"You are the smartest damn animal on the face of the planet. I'm home, and you're going to see a lot more of me than you did the last couple weeks. But I'm going to be inviting people over. Things are going to change around here."

Brady attempted to stand up, and Enemario was on his right side to help to give him the assist. Someone from the front porch ran up and helped on his other side.

"I should have gotten a video of that, God damn it," Riley said. "That was the funniest God damn thing I've ever seen in my life. Tate was all over you. If it was a wrestling match, he'd win. I don't think you're stronger than that dog. He'd whoop your ass anytime."

"Good to see you, Riley. How's the family?"

"Cassie's here. We brought our little group, now that they're not so afraid of the big black dog, and she's getting ready to pop, Brady. So I'm kind of hoping maybe you'll babysit sometime."

"God Almighty, what the hell did I get myself in-to?" Brady whispered. And then he laughed. "You bring them over in your own time. We'll see what we can do. I've got a lot of weeding they can help me with."

"One's just barely walking, and my little girl's three.

You're not going to put them to work yet?"

Brady patted him on the back, disentangled himself from both of his buddies, and said to Riley, "Don't push me. You'd be surprised what a three-year-old can do."

Cassie had brought over one of her friends from the bakery where she used to work. She was a pretty girl, and Brady got the implication immediately they all believed it was time for him to start dating again. As the evening wore on, Brady was very attentive and gentlemanly, but when it got close to ten o'clock, he told the crowd that he was tired, and he needed to go to bed.

He shook everybody's hand, hugged everybody he thought appropriate, gave a small peck on the cheek to the pretty baker from town, and thanked everyone for the warm welcome. Cassie had made some leftovers and stored them in his refrigerator. The boys had bought four cases of beer and left them on the countertop. They informed him Tate had been fed and left his remaining food in the refrigerator and in the garage.

Brady closed the door behind them, surveyed his house, and then retired to the couch where Tate took up his post right next to him.

"God, it's good to be home. Tomorrow, when we can see, we'll check how bad it is out there. No sense spoiling this nice night."

Tate laid his snout on Brady's stomach, giving him an adoring stare.

CHAPTER 19

AS THE WEEKS flew by, Brady consumed himself with making repairs and putting his garden back in order. Weeds had grown to nearly waist high. A leak had formed in the drip irrigation, which created a muddy puddle. His chickens, probably because nobody fed them regularly, had either flown off or been captured by coyotes. His grow wilted and looked like it got infested with spider mites or something coming from the woods. He was surprised nobody took the crop, but he understood it probably didn't look very desirable, either. He spent a day ripping everything out and decided he was done producing the CBD oil.

He didn't want to be tied down to the property so that he couldn't leave ever again. He liked the fact he could put in things and walk away and then come back and find them relatively the same way when he left. Weeds would always grow, irrigation systems would always fail, but he didn't want anybody invading his space or taking care of animals that were overly needy. He was done with all that. There had been a time in his life when it was important he serve his own land, and now he was going to let his land serve him.

He got a call from his mysterious benefactor, requesting he have a meeting with Maggie. She explained to him Maggie had reached out to her several times, and she hadn't wanted to bother him, so she waited until Maggie called one more time. The woman said she could arrange a neutral place for them to meet, if he wanted. Or, if he was okay with it, she could give Maggie Brady's address and invite her to stop by.

Brady paused. This was the moment he knew was coming, eventually. He'd realized he would have to make that decision one day or another, and he decided he would extend the invitation to meet her to talk.

"I'm not saying she can stay over. I'm saying I'm willing to meet her, here or somewhere else. But she used to live in San Diego, and it might be more convenient to meet her there later. I'm not ready to do that yet. But if she wants to come here, I'll allow it."

"Let me suggest an alternative. What if you came down to San Diego and took that little cottage for a few days? We would allow Tate to come with you. Maybe that would be a neutral place to meet, so it wouldn't feel like you had to entertain her?"

Brady thought about that, and perhaps he could be

ready. Besides, after all the hard work he'd put in, he could take a few days at the beach to just kick back.

"Okay, if you set it up, I'll drive down there, and we can have our talk. But make it clear, this is not an overnight thing. I need time to process everything that went on. And I'm sorry if that hurts her. I just need to feel like I'm whole inside before I can start opening that door to friendship again."

"I think that's very wise, Brady. I'll arrange it and give you the details."

Brandy had thought, with the passage of time, Maggie would want to just move on with her life. He couldn't imagine she'd want to relive any of the past, especially the immediate past. She had the chance for a fresh start. So he hadn't been expecting the reach out.

But it did make him wonder why she was so insistent on the meet-and-greet. He didn't think there was anything unresolved or anything that had to be said, and he knew eventually, when things weren't so charged, he'd attend some wedding or funeral or gathering, and she'd be there, and they could talk. That's what he'd figured the future looked like.

In the meantime, he'd be looking to find his next adventure. Not an adventure in warrior terms, but an adventure of the heart. He'd never thought of himself as having a great capacity, but he remembered the story about his friend and his wife and the butterfly.

And he decided that, although he was ready to stop being a warrior, maybe he wasn't ready to give up being a partner. He liked his buddies, and he could see a place in his home and his heart for someone else again.

He just wasn't sure it was Maggie.

On a chilly December day, he and Tate began the trek down to San Diego. They stayed at his favorite midway rest stop, and both ate enormous steaks. Tate sat right next to him on the bench with his own bowl, enjoying the laughter of people in the restaurant as they passed by and saw him there. Then he and Tate made it back into the cab, found a hotel, and rested.

The next morning, the clouds had cleared trailed behind them as they trekked the additional six hours to San Diego. He used his GPS on his brand-new phone, courtesy of the lady, and tracked the little house south of the city in a semi-residential area, dotted with mom-and-pop stores and away from the glitzy beaches and boats of San Diego. It was his kind of place, filled with sand dunes and warm breezy nights. That was one thing he missed living Northern California. The nights were too damn cold!

The house was small, only two bedrooms. Inside, it had been restored but not fully remodeled. Someone had redone the kitchen in knotty pine cabinetry, re-installed retro style Formica, and added old-fashioned aluminum trim, giving the whole place a "back to the 60s" look. It suited him very well. All the furniture inside was generous, overstuffed. There were lots of throws and comforters and a big stone fireplace in the living room with picture windows on both sides of it so you could watch the fire and the waves at the same time.

"Somebody paid close attention to that detail," he said to Tate.

A few staples had been left for him, and a plate of sandwiches waited in the refrigerator covered in plastic. He peeked and grabbed one, handing the other half to Tate who declined.

"You don't like tuna fish, do you?"

About an hour after he had unloaded, he heard a car drive down the driveway. Checking through the lace curtains by the front door, he recognized Maggie in the driver's seat, but she had someone else with her in the back.

"Well, this is not what we agreed to," he said to Tate. Of course she would bend the boundaries, he thought. It annoyed him.

He watched her get out of the car and then walk around to the back door, where he'd spotted the intruder. She leaned into the car and picked up a sleeping child. A little girl. The little girl had long red ringlets, and she was fast asleep on Maggie's shoulder.

Brady's heart stopped. As Maggie walked closer to the front door, her eyes darted to the ground and back up as though she was nervous. He was nervous as well. His hands were shaking, and his armpits shed water like he'd walked out of the shower. But there was no point in delaying this any further, so he opened the door.

Maggie's face was smiling, but the crease between her eyebrows was furrowed. He knew that look. She was trying to put on a brave face, but she was worried.

He stared at the child in her arms. Seconds later, the little girl started to stir.

"Brady, can we come inside?"

He felt like an idiot, "Of course. I'm sorry. I'm—"

Maggie interrupted him. "Brady, there's somebody I'd like you to meet." She turned, with her back facing him, so he could see the face of the little girl. She looked exactly like her mother. Brady was speechless as she opened her eyes. Then she started to squirm so Maggie set her down on the ground. She stood next to her mother, holding hands.

"Brady, this is Emma."

The little girl stared up at him, wiggling the fingers on her right hand and tapping her foot to some imaginary song. Her mother continued. "Emma, this is your father."

When Brady heard the words, he wasn't surprised. The instant he saw the little girl and estimated her age, he realized she probably was his. But hearing it hit him like a ton of bricks. This was the last thing he'd expected.

"Why didn't you tell me?" he asked her.

"I had no way to, and I was stuck. Confused and scared too. He'd threatened to take her away, to *sell* her, Brady, and I'd met women who had that happen to their children. I didn't know what to do, so I opted for keeping her safe. I thought you would be angry. I was in a very tough situation. The day she came into this world, I vowed I would do whatever I could to keep her safe. That was my primary concern. I hoped that someday you would get to meet her. But I'm not asking you for anything, not even forgiveness."

He wasn't going to show it, but his insides were melting, his whole defense system shutting down, dripping and shriveling like an ice cave in summer. He was teetering on the edge, wondering which way he would fall…and then he decided.

Brady knelt to the floor and addressed Emma. He held out his hand. "Emma, it's nice to meet you. Did you have a good trip?"

The little girl didn't take his hand but hid behind Maggie's skirt. She poked her head around the corner and peered at him, her innocent, unsmiling face studying his.

He stood up. "That's okay. It's kind of a lot to take in. I suppose she's not used to the idea of being introduced to…"

"On the contrary, she's seen your picture, Brady. She knows a lot about you. I've told her. But she's scared."

Maggie's lower lip began to tremble as tears spilled from her eyes.

Brady nodded. His body responded in reflex, his eyes also filling up with water. "She's not the only one. Maggie—"

She fell into his arms, and at first, it was awkward. His mind screamed he wasn't ready. Then suddenly he was filled with the familiar scent of her hair and her body, the yearning of the years he'd missed her, the joy of the year they spent together, and the desire of the fantasy dreams he'd survived on the past three years. He could feel her shaking. He also noticed Emma hugged the two of them, wanting to be included.

Brady felt he was at precipice, one of those high dive rocks he used to jump off when he was a kid. Just like on those endless summer days, it was time to vault off the ledge, scare himself senseless, and fly.

He knew he wasn't quite ready, but he chose the

excitement, jitters and all, and jumped anyway.

He kissed Maggie on the ear and whispered, "I am so glad you're back."

CHAPTER 20

L IGHT HIT BRADY'S face, gently drawing him out of his slumber. His reflex was always to go back into the dream, to prolong the fantasy for as long as he could. He played tug of war, keeping his eyes closed and feeling the touch of her firm, smooth flesh beneath his fingertips. Her breathing pressed her chest into his, covering him with the lightness of her being, sending his senses into overload.

Keeping his eyes closed, his fingers clutched at the roots of her glorious, copper-colored hair, telling her non-verbally of his need.

Her hand pressed down the side of his body, over his hip, and found him, fully engorged and ready.

"Again?" she sighed.

But this was different. He opened his eyes, and she was still there. They were wrapped together in a sheet, legs entangled from their foreplay, after play, and all the glorious minutes in between. The bed smelled like them both. The sounds of gentle waves corresponded with her breath. Sea birds called out as she spread her legs, pulled herself up, and rubbed her pubic bone down his shaft. Hard.

It was real.

He flipped her on her back, breached her opening slowly, and watched her wince and tear up from the pain, the wounding he'd caused her from a whole night of lovemaking. God how he loved seeing her accept him, grow in her desire, crescendo into something beautiful and wild, pushing against him holding his leg with hers, undulating and begging for him to do deeper, give her more.

As his rhythm increased, he rocked her softly, kissing her breasts and pressing her closer with his hand beneath the small of her back. Her knees bent, accepting him deeper. He whispered in her ear his first truth of the day. "God, I can't get enough of you."

She stopped, and he opened his eyes, staring down at her face. She looked to the side, behind him. He turned quickly and saw Emma standing there, watching them both.

Brady scrambled to cover himself up, which exposed Maggie's breasts to her daughter. He grabbed the sheets and covered her up hastily, but then he felt his rear exposed, so he quickly flipped over.

Little Emma watched this stoically and then said,

"What are you doing to Mommy?"

"Sweetheart, he's giving me a massage."

"But he's naked."

"That's how it's done between adults sometimes," Maggie answered. "Everything is fine, sweetheart. I'm sorry if it made you worry."

Emma looked down at Tate, who looked right back at her, as if agreeing. Her sweet little voice directed the dog as though they were long friends. "Come on, Tate. Let's go play in the other room."

Without looking back, Emma turned and walked out, Tate right beside her.

Brady shook his head, rubbed his fingers through his hair, and pulled. Everything felt the same, tasted and smelled the same, but it was all different. He was embarrassed and wouldn't look at Maggie.

"Not your fault," she whispered to his lips, touching him lightly under his chin. She was casually seated crosswise, her body leaning into his chest. She kissed the side of his neck. Her fair fell against his shoulder; her breasts moved against his upper arm.

He found the tears welling up inside him, missing the years they had lost, the pain and horror she'd seen while he was feeling sorry for himself, arming himself for Armageddon. He marveled how strong she had been to keep little Emma safe.

She kissed first his right eyelid and then his left.

"Stay with me, Brady. Let me take care of you. I'm never ever going to leave again. Let me prove my love for you. I need your strength too. We need you in our lives, forever."

It did little to stop the crying, but he let them flow anyway. She laid him back on the bed, whispering things he'd heard before but loving them even more now. Her body carefully, delicately, and with all the passion in her soul wrapped around him and drew him back to life.

In her arms, he remembered what he wanted to do.

He wanted to live forever, be a family, and love like no one was watching.

Now he realized that to truly have her and appreciate the gift of her love, he had to lose her first.

Did you enjoy Shadow of the Heart? If so, I'd love to hear it! You can contact me at: sharon@authorsharonhamilton.com

But wait! Maybe you're a new reader of mine. Maybe you want to fall in love all over again with the original SEAL stories that made Sharon famous? Be sure to read the bundle with the first five books in the SEAL Brotherhood Series, the Ultimate SEAL Collection #1, from the series that started it all. Included in this bundle are two novellas. You can check these out or read more about them or the audio books attached to them.

And be sure to read all the other authors who wrote in this Shadow SEALs Series. Some have already been published and some you can preorder now. Check them out by going to this link here authorsharonhamilton.com/shadow-seals

ABOUT THE AUTHOR

 NYT and USA/Today Bestselling Author Sharon Hamilton's SEAL Brotherhood series have earned her author rankings of #1 in Romantic Suspense, Military Romance and Contemporary Romance. Her other *Brotherhood* stand-alone series are: Bad Boys of SEAL Team 3, Band of Bachelors, True Blue SEALs, Nashville SEALs, Bone Frog Brotherhood, Sunset SEALs, Bone Frog Bachelor Series and SEAL Brotherhood Legacy Series. She is a contributing author to the very popular Shadow SEALs multi-author series.

Her SEALs and former SEALs have invested in two wineries, a lavender farm and a brewery in Sonoma County, which have become part of the new stories. They also have expanded to include Veteran-benefit projects on the Florida Gulf Coast, as well as projects in Africa and the Maldives. One of the SEAL wives has even launched her own women's fiction series. But old characters, as well as children of these SEAL heroes keep returning to all the newer books.

Sharon also writes sexy paranormals in two series: Golden Vampires of Tuscany and The Guardians.

A lifelong organic vegetable and flower gardener, Sharon and her husband lived for fifty years in the Wine Country of Northern California, where many of her stories take place. Recently, they have moved to the beautiful Gulf Coast of Florida, with stories of shipwrecks, the white sugar-sand beaches of Sunset, Treasure Island and Indian Rocks Beaches.

She loves hearing from fans through her website: authorsharonhamilton.com

Find out more about Sharon, her upcoming releases, appearances and news when you sign up for Sharon's newsletter.

Facebook:
facebook.com/SharonHamiltonAuthor

Twitter:
twitter.com/sharonlhamilton

Pinterest:
pinterest.com/AuthorSharonH

Amazon:
amazon.com/Sharon-Hamilton/e/B004FQQMAC

BookBub:
bookbub.com/authors/sharon-hamilton

Youtube:
youtube.com/channel/UCDInkxXFpXp_4Vnq08ZxMBQ

Soundcloud:
soundcloud.com/sharon-hamilton-1

Sharon Hamilton's Rockin' Romance Readers:
facebook.com/groups/sealteamromance

Sharon Hamilton's Goodreads Group:
goodreads.com/group/show/199125-sharon-hamilton-
readers-group

Visit Sharon's Online Store:
sharon-hamilton-author.myshopify.com

Join Sharon's Review Teams:

eBook Reviews:
sharonhamiltonassistant@gmail.com

Audio Reviews:
sharonhamiltonassistant@gmail.com

Life is one fool thing after another.
Love is two fool things after each other.

REVIEWS

PRAISE FOR THE
GOLDEN VAMPIRES OF TUSCANY SERIES

"Well to say the least I was thoroughly surprise. I have read many Vampire books, from Ann Rice to Kym Grosso and few other Authors, so yes I do like Vampires, not the super scary ones from the old days, but the new ones are far more interesting far more human than one can remember. I found Honeymoon Bite a totally engrossing book, I was not able to put it down, page after page I found delight, love, understanding, well that is until the bad bad Vamp started being really bad. But seeing someone love another person so much that they would do anything to protect them, well that had me going, then well there was more and for a while I thought it was the end of a beautiful love story that spanned not only time but, spanned Italy and California. Won't divulge how it ended, but I did shed a few tears after screaming but Sharon Hamilton did not let me down, she took me on amazing trip that I loved, look forward to reading another Vampire book of hers."

"An excellent paranormal romance that was exciting, romantic, entertaining and very satisfying to read. It had me anticipating what would happen next many times over, so much so I could not put it down and even finished it up in a day. The vampires in this book were different from your average vampire, but I enjoy different variations and changes to the same old stuff. It made for a more unpredictable read and more adventurous to explore! Vampire lovers, any paranormal readers and even those who love the romance genre will enjoy Honeymoon Bite."

"This is the first non-Seal book of this author's I have read and I loved it. There is a cast-like hierarchy in this vampire community with humans at the very bottom and Golden vampires at the top. Lionel is a dark vampire who are servants of the Goldens. Phoebe is a Golden who has not decided if she will remain human or accept the turning to become a vampire. Either way she and Lionel can never be together since it is forbidden.

I enjoyed this story and I am looking forward to the next installment."

"A hauntingly romantic read. Old love lost and new love found. Family, heart, intrigue and vampires. Grabbed my attention and couldn't put down. Would definitely recommend."

PRAISE FOR THE
SEAL BROTHERHOOD SERIES

"Fans of Navy SEAL romance, I found a new author to feed your addiction. Finely written and loaded delicious with moments, Sharon Hamilton's storytelling satisfies like a thick bar of chocolate." —Marliss Melton, bestselling author of the *Team Twelve* Navy SEALs series

"Sharon Hamilton does an EXCELLENT job of fitting all the characters into a brotherhood of SEALS that may not be real but sure makes you feel that you have entered the circle and security of their world. The stories intertwine with each book before...and each book after and THAT is what makes Sharon Hamilton's SEAL Brotherhood Series so very interesting. You won't want to put down ANY of her books and they will keep you reading into the night when you should be sleeping. Start with this book...and you will not want to stop until you've read the whole series and then...you will be waiting for Sharon to write the next one." (5 Star Review)

"Kyle and Christy explode all over the pages in this first book, *[Accidental SEAL]*, in a whole new series of SEALs. If the twist and turns don't get your heart jumping, then maybe the suspense will. This is a must read for those that are looking for love and adventure with a little sloppy love thrown in for good measure." (5 Star Review)

PRAISE FOR THE
BAD BOYS OF SEAL TEAM 3 SERIES

"I love reading this series! Once you start these books, you can hardly put them down. The mix of romance and suspense keeps you turning the pages one right after another! Can't wait until the next book!" (5 Star Review)

"I love all of Sharon's Seal books, but *[SEAL's Code]* may just be her best to date. Danny and Luci's journey is filled with a wonderful insight into the Native American life. It is a love story that will fill you with warmth and contentment. You will enjoy Danny's journey to become a SEAL and his reasons for it. Good job Sharon!" (5 Star Review)

PRAISE FOR THE
BAND OF BACHELORS SERIES

"*[Lucas]* was the first book in the Band of Bachelors series and it was a phenomenal start. I loved how we got to see the other SEALs we all love and we got a look at Lucas and Marcy. They had an instant attraction, and their love was very intense. This book had it all, suspense, steamy romance, humor, everything you want in a riveting, outstanding read. I can't wait to read the next book in this series." (5 Star Review)

PRAISE FOR THE
TRUE BLUE SEALS SERIES

"Keep the tissues box nearby as you read *True Blue SEALs: Zak* by Sharon Hamilton. I imagine more than I wish to that the circumstances surrounding Zak and Amy are all too real for returning military personnel and their families. Ms. Hamilton has put us right in the middle of struggles and successes that these two high school sweethearts endure. I have read several of Sharon Hamilton's military romances but will say this is the most emotionally intense of the ones that I have read. This is a well-written, realistic story with authentic characters that will have you rooting for them and proud of those who serve to keep us safe. This is an author who writes amazing stories that you love and cry with the characters. Fans of Jessica Scott and Marliss Melton will want to add Sharon Hamilton to their list of realistic military romance writers." (5 Star Review)

"Dear FATHER IN HEAVEN,

If I may respectfully say so sometimes you are a strange God. Though you love all mankind,

It seems you have special predilections too.

You seem to love those men who can stand up alone who face impossible odds, Who challenge every bully and every tyrant ~

Those men who know the heat and loneliness of Calvary. Possibly you cherish men of this stamp because you recognize the mark of your only son in them.

Since this unique group of men known as the SEALs know Calvary and suffering, teach them now the mystery of the resurrection ~ that they are indestructible, that they will live forever because of their deep faith in you.

And when they do come to heaven, may I respectfully warn you, Dear Father, they also know how to celebrate. So please be ready for them when they insert under your pearly gates.

Bless them, their devoted Families and their Country on this glorious occasion.

We ask this through the merits of your Son, Christ Jesus the Lord, Amen."

By Reverend E.J. McMalhon S.J. LCDR, CHC, USN
Awards Ceremony SEAL Team One
1975 At NAB, Coronado